Here are other books by Mike Haynes-Pitts

The Surge Series: The Way to Akom on Amazon

The Surge Series: Harvesters' Diaspora on Amazon

The Surge Series
Book 1 - Second Edition – Pulse of the City

Written and Edited Mike Haynes-Pitts

Cover art by Atagun Ilhan

FOREWORD

The intention of this foreword is to be quick. I want to leave the initial foreword here to give thanks to those that inspired my early attempts at writing. However, since this is the 2nd edition and I have since made a whole trilogy of Afrofuturistic, Black Femme LGBTQ cyberpunk stories, I have brand new perspectives. I want to give a shout out and thanks to anyone who has ever read, enjoyed, helped or inspired the Surge Series trilogy. I hope you truly love this re-edited book that aligns better with the trilogy and my writing now.

And while this is a new foreword, here are some of the old shout outs. I have so much gratitude for Patricia D'Empaire, now Gyapong, for the initial reviewing and helping edit this novella. Lacuna D'Empaire gets her namesake from you and so much more. I want to give thanks to Lorena Candelario for inspiring Ramirez, Spanish assistance and many Dominican Republic cultural aspects for Machado and Ramirez. I also have many thanks to my cyberpunk counterpart Nikolas Weiss for all the talk of Cyberpunk 2077, Edgerunners and a whole lot of literature. Lastly, I give thanks to Jayde McDougle for constantly marketing and being in my corner for this trilogy. For those of you who know Noreita from Book 3, Jayde is the inspiration.

The History of the Surge

Most people forgot about the time before the Surge. However, many historians keep up with the chronological calendar and time of events. While the calendar of time is based on Christianity, most no longer believe in religion since it happened. It was a cataclysmic event that changed both class systems and world balance. Much of the AI of the world was irrevocably damaged and many economic foundations collapsed. Some theorized it was the work of aliens while others thought it was a singularity. As it stands, Africa has become one of the most prominent regions of the world. Most descendants from the land returned in a sort of reverse diaspora. This return would create a dystopian world in the megacities of Africa.

One of the largest of these in West Africa is Accra in Ghana. Ran by military police, gangs and the wealthy elite, Accra is where everyone wants to be, but no one can afford to be. In the years after the Surge, Surge candidates, those imbued with strange electric auras would undoubtedly change the fate of the world.

<u>Prologue</u>

2336. Tesano Municipality in Accra, Ghana. Five years after the Surge.

Tesano. The land of the 1000 gangs. While there are only thirteen gangs, most citizens think there are so many gang members there might as well be a thousand gangs. Filled with tight alleys and fairly tall buildings, it's a treacherous city. No cameras, no military and very few stable places. Still, there's plenty of business. Amongst the neon lights there are brothels, "drug" stores, and several illegal weapon shops. Smells from all manner of scum and villainy fester in these illicit dens. Throughout the streets, the music of the Techno Kids' gang pulses on every corner. In the Northwest region of Tesano lies the Harvesters. The Harvesters are known for their smuggling and cyberware. They are one of the strongest gangs in the region. On this particular night, the Harvesters discuss a newfound Surge candidate to add to their gang. In attendance are the leaders of the Harvester gang. The first is Machado Ramirez, the leader of the Harvesters, is a man of average height with brown skin and cyberware. He also has a beard and flat top fade. His sister, who also leads, is known as Ramirez. She is darker skinned than him. She has long locs and a muscular frame intertwined with cyberware. Lacuna D'Empaire, who is second in command after the Ramirez siblings, has darker skin than both of them. She is slim and tall with long grey locs. Also in attendance are the Harvesters lead technical genius and computer expert Xochitl Camal. She is average height with long hair. She has brown skin that has several digitally enhanced Aztec tattoos. Lastly, is the American-born, Greene, who repairs cyberware and manages the general Harvesters. He is similar in stature to Machado. He is bald with a slight beard and medium brown skin.

Lacuna announces news to the group.

"This Surge candidate in Kumasi has some of the strongest readings ever. Lucius Baker said the Conduit has never peaked so high. Not even for me. I have a feeling they'll be a great addition to the Harvesters."

Machado replies with doubt.

"You think so? Hmmm either way we'll have to initiate them. "

Ramirez adds an idea to his.

"Ey hermano, maybe we take them on a body mod run. The Cloaks' supply factory is nearby Kumasi."

Xochitl questions the whole process.

"You think she'll join after that? Didn't you say we needed to convince them to go against their family?"

Machado states it will be no issue.

"That will be no problem once Lacuna meets them. I'm sure they'll be so fascinated; they'll ally with us. Greene, hold down the headquarters. "

Greene confirms his command.

"No problem bro. See y'all soon."

End of Prologue

****

Chapter 1

Kumasi, Ghana

Bathed in moonlight, my state-of-the-art new home sits on the outskirts of Kumasi. Each floor is spread out with a variety of African sculptures and decorations. State-of-the-art technology protects the entire home. It is the home of my family, the Osuwus. My mother and father are renown military doctors for the Asante Kingdom. My brother, Kwaku, is studying to be a professor at the military university. Meanwhile I, Afia, am studying Forensics at the university. However, I often find myself more into research on breakthroughs of the Surge. I do this research because I am a Surge candidate with fascinating powers. I can manipulate electric currents. Only my brother knows of my power. We keep it a secret from everyone, including our parents. If the military learns of my power, they will want it as a weapon or to send me to the slums. In the slums are where many poor Surge candidates stay. There are almost no chances for them to obtain jobs. The reason for this is that the Asante military General, General Aku, hates Surge candidates. She keeps the slum-dwellers and most Surge candidates under her boot.

I hope that one day I can move to Accra. The research for Surge and the job opportunities are far greater there. While I ponder my future, I hear a knock on my window. I peer out to see a swirl of blue Surge energy. The sight entrances me. I walk closer and see an older woman with dark skin like me under the moon's glow. Thoughts race through my head on what to do next. Ultimately, I open the window and the lady enters politely.

Lacuna introduces herself.
"Greetings, my name is Lacuna. I'm a long-time candidate of Surge. I've been searching for you. "

My excitement is palpable.
"You have the Surge too?! That's probably how you got through the security systems outside. I thought it was only me and some of those Regiment people in Kumasi. Can't believe you have that much power!"

Lacuna explains more about the Surge.
"There's more of us than you think. I don't think you fully grasp the power you have. As such, would you like to learn more control and ideas around your powers?"

The possibility greatly interests me.
"You would do that? Can you teach me? How?! My brother will be so excited to…"

She stops me right there.
"No we can't do that… What is your name?"

I reply with confusion.
"Afia Osuwu. Why not?"

She says to be on guard.
"Afia, we must not tell your family yet. We have an important mission for you to learn some more Surge powers first."

I question her about the others with her.
"Who is this we?"

She states *who they are.*
"My teammates."

She produces a holovid showcasing Machado, Ramirez, Xochitl and various Harvesters.

I notice all the tech that grafts into their bodies.
"They have a lot of cyber gear in their bodies. They remind me of some gang I read about."

She reassures me.
"Not to worry Afia. In time, you can learn more about me and my team. More importantly, you'll get to learn about the Surge. But first, my teammates need to see if you're worthy. You'll have to help us get body mods."

I ask with uncertainty. .

"You want me to get body mods? Why don't you just go and handle it? "She ponders for a moment. "Wait…you want me to steal?"

She soothes me.

"You don't have to do anything but stick with me and learn. I've always taken care of my own. Afia, it's now or never." She gets up to leave out the window.

I follow her. I glance back at my home.

I say out loud.

"I hope my family won't worry. Let me put on my coat and let's go join this group of yours."

End Chapter 1

****

Chapter 2

We arrive at a modified, low, hovercar. Outside of the transport are Xochitl, Ramirez, and Machado.

Ramirez introduces herself to me.
"My my, Lacuna, I didn't know our Surge candidate would be so cute. Hey there, I'm Ramirez. This is mi hermano and leader of our crew, Machado. And this is our tech and body mod specialist, Xochitl."
Xochitl takes a break from her work.
"Mucho Gusto."
I realize just what criminals I'm talking to.
"The Machado Ramirez?!?! The leader of the Harvesters?! Lacuna, I thought you weren't in a gang."

I turn back to Lacuna for answers.

She looks away.
"I..."
Machado walks up to me.
"Afia, is it? Let me explain. I started the Harvesters long ago to take advantage of body modification. We did this to keep the mods out of the hands of the oppressive military and other criminals. All our efforts help fund our communities overseas. The Surge hit the Caribbean hard. Africa on the other hand, was a land of opportunity."
I think about his explanation.
"Well, that does explain the rise in refugees. Still, you all have committed crimes."
Machado sighs and tires to put me at ease.
"We do what we must. As does anyone these days. However, if you want to learn more about your powers, you roll with me."

He puts his arm around me and gives me a knowing wink.

I eventually agree to his ideas.
"True. Fine, I'll go along for now."
Lacuna smiles at my decision.
"Glad to see it. Now, Machado, she's pretty new. She can probably only give us sparks at best."
Machado walks to the hovercar.
"Estas no problemo. I have faith in your teaching!"
Ramirez pulls me away from her brother.
"Vamos, mi amor come sit next to me."

I blush deeply before going into the hovercar. Ramirez is the most attractive woman I know. I'm in awe that she's into me. Xochitl watches Ramirez and I exchange glances. She shrugs and sets off for a supply factory near Kejetia Market. The factory is ran by the Cloaks, a gang who specializes fight with vibro-blades. They also use cloaks for stealth and assassinations. The gang consists of mainly northern-Ghana tribes and African-Americans. The Cloaks frequently clash with the Harvesters.

I wonder about our destination.
"Where are we headed?"
Xochitl replies *to my query.*
"We're going to grab some cyber gear from this supply factory. Maybe we'll see how your powers are with security."

I grimace at the thought of attempting to get through security.

Lacuna calms my nerves.
"C'est bien. I can handle a great deal of the security, but I will show you how to open and bypass doors. You have much to learn."
Ramirez flirts in earnest with me.

"After that, maybe you can try some Surge on me. Just kidding, Lacuna. Don't give me that look."

Lacuna laughs at her flirtations. Xochitl groans.

Xochitl berates Ramirez.
"Do you ever stop with the newbies, Ramirez? You just met the woman and you're making moves."
She claps back.
"Diablo! Don't act like if the candidate was a man, you wouldn't be interested."
Lacuna states some new information for everyone.
"Afia has a brother. Kwaku, was it?"
I reply that I do.
"Yes, but he has no Surge."
Ramirez laughs at his of powers.
"So he's not as useful as you."
Xochitl comments on Ramirez's constant nonsense.
"Mierde Ramirez, you know I like all men or women. Still, maybe learn about new people before you date them. Si o no?"
Machado interrupts everyone for an update.
"Alright, we're nearing the factory. Todo silencio and get ready. Xochitl put up the tracker screen. The rest of you turn your frequencies on. Hermana, you're with me. Lacuna, show Afia some new skills then come join me."

We get out of the hovercar. Xochitl hides the hovercar in the trees then prepares her tech station. Machado and Ramirez grab a few packs from the hovercar for supplies. Then, we head to the supply factory. Lacuna motions me forward. She shows me how to bypass the door. She prompts me to conjure a weak spark of Surge.

She tells me.
"Concentrate. This should become a simple task for you. The other ones will take time, but this one I know you can do."

I close my eyes and make a large spark that short circuits the security door. Lacuna sighs but still applauds my efforts. Machado and Ramirez enter. They ready their body modification blades. The sharp blades split open from their arms.

Lacuna encourages me.
"That was not a bad start. Now watch as I use the Surge to hit all of the security in the building. Go wait by Xochitl's tracking system. Now pay attention. This will be fun."

She gathers a great deal of Surge in her. She concentrates her energy on the factory. She sends a large pulse through it. The whole factory shuts off from her EMP pulse. The production in the factory stalls. The skeleton working crew achieves bewilderment at the pause in production. Lacuna joins Machado and Ramirez in the factory. I stay behind with Xochitl.

I marvel at her tech.
"Anything I can do to help, tech wise?"
She shrugs off my assistance.
"You barely have control of your powers. Don't short circuit my computer. But keep a lookout and watch the trackers on Manuela. You'll learn eventually."
I don't see anyone around us. I ask who that could be.
"Who's Manuela?"
She whirls around pats her computer.
"It's this baby right here. It's all I have left after that puta Ramirez broke my babies Yanaira and Rosaria."

I give her a quizzical look.

She stares back blankly.

"Hey, we all love something. I love computers. Now, let's see what is going on."

Lacuna, Machado and Ramirez search the darkened supply factory. The smell of oil, steel and electricity lingers in the air. The factory is silent except a few Cloaks due to the stalled machinery. The three Harvesters move past the conveyor belts looking for the product storage room. Lacuna sends Surge to set off a conveyor belt. Several Cloaks attend to the source of the noise. In the commotion, the Harvesters are able to get to the storage room. Lacuna bypasses the storage door with Surge. A Cloak in the room hears the door open and sees them. Machado quickly silences the guard with one of his arm blades. Ramirez loads one of the packs they brought with cyber implants and body modifications. Lacuna helps her. Machado hides the body of the Cloak. While they work, a guard sees the storage door open. The guard rushes to the alarm. Machado attempts to stop him, but it's too late. As the alarm goes off, Xochitl's voice buzzes through the Harvesters' frequency.

She clamors at everyone.
"Guys get out now! The alarm is blaring! I'm already tracking a swarm of Cloaks closing in!"

Lacuna jumpstarts another conveyor belt with robotic arms. The arms short circuit and wave around in every direction. The Cloaks fire vibro-guns and throw laser daggers. In the confusion, they aim towards the Harvesters and the robotic arms. Ramirez and Machado bring out their robotic exoskeletons to shield themselves from the projectiles. The three Harvesters flee from the factory. Ramirez drops a bag of gear while rushing to the hovercar. She curses to herself but manages to still get three bags out. Xochitl starts up the hovercar. I analyze Manuela to see signs of the Harvesters.

One of the backup Cloaks spots the hovercar. He sprints to stop it with his sword. I freak out and fire a quick Surge spark to the guard's sword, which electrocutes him. The other three Harvesters arrive at the hovercar. A hail of laser daggers penetrates the hovercar. The remaining Cloaks try to block the hovercar.

Machado yells at Xochitl to get going.
"Punch it Xochitl!!!"
Xochitl slams on the car's thrusters.
"Already happening!"

The hovercar lifts over the Cloaks. We zoom away toward Kejetia Market.

End Chapter 2
****

<u>Chapter 3</u>

In a small open-air bar, we laugh and enjoy the spoils from the factory. The bar is in Kejetia Market, one of the prime trading spots in Kumasi. The market contains all kinds of activity. Vendors selling wares through holopads. The sounds of hawkers bringing customers to their stalls. And the smells of fresh cocoa churning into chocolate. The sweet aroma of palm wine fills the bar. Machado reaches for a glass for a toast.

Machado toasts to our success.
"Not too bad Afia. It would be nice to have another Surge candidate on our team."
Ramirez joins in.
"Bueno. I loved when you shocked that Cloak's sword."
I am unsure at my accidental skill.
"Not sure how I did it, but I'm just glad you're all ok."

I eye Ramirez when I say this. Then I focus on the rest of the team.

Lacuna leans forward.
"If you managed to pull that off, then I have so much more I can teach you. I can't wait to show you everything. Who knows, I might have to start calling you the Voidess. "
We stare at her in disbelief. She delights at our concern.
"D'accord. I'm the only Voidess. But you're really good Afia. This is great."
I question who the Voidess is.
"Voidess? Sounds good on you Lacuna. Hah you and me Lacuna; all the power of the Surge voiding people out."
Ramirez see my eyes glaze over and shakes her head.
"Easy there."

Xochitl agrees that I'm not fully ready.
"I'm glad you helped me back there. I truly appreciate it, Afia. But I still hate that we lost a bag of cyber implants."
Machado waves the loss off.
"It's ok we'll manage. Now Afia, we need to talk about what you need to do to join us."
I gasp at there being more to it.
"What do you mean? I thought that was it."
He explains the whole story.
"Well, my assumption is that you enjoyed this and you want Lacuna to teach you more. In order to be with us we need those blueprint documents from your home. We want more Surge candidates, but we need those."
Ramirez adds on to his story.
"Furthermore, your family has done the best cyber research around. Xochitl and our guy back home, Greene will use those blueprints to help us. No more surprises after this."
My confusion remains.
"Wait, but I thought…"

I look at Lacuna. She looks back nervously. What in the Orishas am I doing?

She explains her side.
"It was part of the deal of getting you. We need that research to improve the Harvesters. And it's also to help the man that gave information to you."
I calm down a bit.
"Ok, ok. Let me think about it. I'll need to figure out how to get to it."
Xochitl interludes my thinking with a tool to help.
"Bien. Take this encryption spike. It should work to help through any automated security you have."
Machado ends the conversation with his frequency.

"My frequency is L-314. If I'm not available right away, I'll transfer the frequency to one of us."

Ramirez rubs my back.

"Don't worry. We're not leaving you."

Lacuna acknowledges their advice. We return to Xochitl's hovercar to go back to my home.

End Chapter 3

****

Chapter 4

The House of the Osuwus.

When we land at my house, there is a downpour of rain. The fresh scent of wet leaves filters through our senses. I exit the hovercar on my own. The Harvesters wait for me to complete their mission. I enter my home late at night and go into the basement. There lies a secret door that leads to where my parents hold some of their medical blueprints. I attempt what Lacuna told me about hacking doors with the Surge. It works a little too well and fries the circuits on the door. I pause to contemplate my future. Once I join the Harvesters, there is no going back. I do not know when I will see my parents again. I am uncertain if this is the right choice, but I need to figure that out for myself. I send a prayer to the Orishas and grab the blueprints for the self-healing limbs. As I'm leaving, my mother stands at the door.

She is barely awake.
"Afia. What is this? Why are you in here? It's so late. What are you doing down here at this hour?"
I shudder while I explain.
"Mama. Pay no heed. It's not important. I'm sorry but I have to go."
She pursues me as I leave.
"Wait Afia. Your father is coming down. You need to answer for yourself this instant."

My dad comes down the stairs. His tall frame blocks my escape.

He demands me to confess.
"Afia, what the hell is this?! I called the military police because I thought someone was breaking in. Explain yourself."

I plead with him.
"Baba, I have to go. There's no time. I'll explain everything later. I have to do this. It's going to get me farther than the university."

He remains obstinate.
"Afia, hand me those documents at once! You don't know what you're doing. Stop this foolishness at once.

I try to shove through my parents, but they block me. I try a second attempt. My efforts do nothing, and I become frustrated. In my anger and determination, I send out a Surge spark. It knocks my parents unconscious. I am horrified. I falter to my knees at the sight of my actions.

I cry while kneeling over them.
"O no! Mama, Baba. What have I done…?!"

Lacuna patches into my frequency.
"Afia, what was that Surge blast? I'm near your house. Are you ok?"

I remain saddened.
"It's my parents. The Surge hit and I think I hurt them really bad."

She calms me.
"Your parents will be fine. My Surge is detecting that they are still breathing."

I realize that somehow, she can monitor my Surge.
"Wait, you followed me? You can see the details of my Surge?"

She explains more about who we are.
"I knew this would be rough. I told Machado I would monitor you. In time, you will notice those details through the Surge as well. Your parents are ok, but you won't be if the police get you. Whose energy is that moving towards you?"

I hear footsteps coming down to join me. It is my brother, Kwaku. He sees me over our unconscious parents. At first, he is in shock. Then he grabs a machete from the hallway and points it at me.

I beg my brother to understand.
"Kwaku, I can explain everything. They're ok. It was an accident."
Kwaku raises his machete.
"Get the hell out Afia! I don't know what you've done, but I will hurt you if you stay here!"
I weep bitterly in that I can't get through to him.
"Kwaku, they're not dead. My Surge power must have made them go to sleep."
Kwaku is too angry to see otherwise and ignores me.
"Of course. I knew you'd use them for evil. Get out now!"
I stammer and the words barely come out.
Kwaku please."
Kwaku roars and advances to me.
"Get out before I kill you!"

I sprint out of my house with the blueprints. Lacuna waits for me outside. I fall into her arms and sob quietly. She consoles me and holds me up. We walk away from the house and towards the Harvester hovercar.

End Chapter 4
****

Chapter 5

We drive Xochitl's hovercar to a military transport hovercraft that is going to Accra. We situate ourselves in the stern compartment of the vessel. We discuss the blueprint plans. Meanwhile, Lacuna trains me.

Machado speaks to Xochitl about the blueprints.
"Xochitl. Can you do anything with these blueprints?
Xochitl thinks and suggests.
"I'll see what I can do. I'll need my equipment back in Accra to fully do anything. I should be able to rewire at least a cyber arm or two to be self-healing. I'll experiment."

On the other side of the compartment are where Lacuna and I practice with the Surge.

Lacuna reminds me to concentrate.
"Concentrate Afia. You should be able to trace movement energy now. Replay my instructions in your mind. Project your Surge."

I materialize a blue outline of me and Lacuna's path. She highlights it with a stronger spark of Surge.

She grins at my progress.
"See Afia. Now you can sense information in the Surge. Next, we can start pushing you to read and manipulate tech waves. You'll be, as some people say, a technocrat."
I ponder about her predictions.
"Like the real Voidess."
She is amused.
"Maybe."

Ramirez saunters over in admiration of me. She applauds my skill.

She proclaims.
"Hell yeah! You're an absolute badass Afia. It's pretty hot."

I slip off guard by the compliment. I lose my concentration and the outline disappears.

Lacuna takes a deep breath.
"Ramirez. Please hold that mouth of yours while we train. Be thankful I even let you watch us practice."
She rolls her eyes.
"Sorry sis. Whatever you say. Guess I'll move along."
I interject between them.
"Ramirez. It's fine. We'll hang when we get to Accra. Maybe you can show me a great place to eat."
She feigns surprise.
"Que? Well then Afia, it's a date! Now Lacuna, please continue."
Lacuna refocuses both of us.
"Ladies, can we get back to work please!"

My training resumes. The hovercraft transport makes its way into the airport of Accra. Accra's tall downtown business skyscrapers contrast the military forts and suburbs of Kumasi. The airport buzzes with the commotion of families, military police and businesspeople. Accra continues to be one of the only stable regions of West Africa since the Surge. Many foreigners come here for trade, crime and business. At the arrival gate, there are more Harvesters waiting for us. Greene, the manager of the Harvesters, greets us.

He beams with excitement.
"Xochitl, Lacuna, Ramirez over here! So good to see you. And hello young lady. Who might you be?"
Ramirez is protective of me.
"Her name is Afia. She's with me."

He puts his hands up in response.

"Take it easy Ramirez. You know I'm not interested in ladies. No time to catch up though. Machado, we gotta talk."

Machado questions him.

"What's up Greene? We had a long trip. We need to put this gear into storage."

Greene is coy. Then he explains the dilemma.

"Well boss. The Cloaks heard about the supply run you just made. They think and probably know it's us. Sister Solace will want to rumble. It's going to be happening near headquarters. I gathered up some melee weapons to keep the military off our backs. Still, you never know with Solace and her Cloaks."

Machado is upset.

"Diablo! Greene! I thought we were good?!"

Greene wards off any concern.

"Minor setback. What did you bring in the meantime?"

Machado gives in.

"We got some new cyber gear for implants. Xochitl got a sweet new blueprint. And we may have a new weapon. But right now it looks like that's all going to have to wait huh?"

Greene laughs at him.

"Hey man, we did our best but you know how the Cloaks are. Let's get back quickly. I want to be ready for those bastards."

End Chapter 5

****

Chapter 6

We wind through the buildings in the hovercar to the Harvester headquarters. When we get there, Harvesters surround the hovercar to bring in the stolen warehouse gear. Greene tells the other Harvesters to prepare for a rumble. The rest of us return to the headquarters while Machado gives orders.

He shouts to his gang.
"Harvesters! It's good to be back home!"

They roar in approval of their leader.

He continues his speech.
"Companeros, we brought cyber gear, designs and some human power. But we don't have much time, those Cloaks will be here soon. Grab the close-range weapons and meet us outside for a rumble!"

They roar in unison and prepare their cyberware. The sounds of the Harvesters cyber implants whir and clang in unison. Several Harvesters pass by me on the way to grab blunt weapons.

I ask out to whoever is listening.
"What's a rumble?"
Ramirez leans into me.
"My favorite. A good pre-Surge street brawl. No guns, just fists and melee weapons. Sometimes blades, sometimes not. With the Cloaks it will be blades, but I think they'll only be on stun."
My face rises in consternation.
"You THINK they'll be on stun? So they could kill? People die?!"
Lacuna steps in.

"We try to avoid it if we can. This is often done to show we're not cowards. No one can take our territory. However, you and I will be in the back checking for any guns or extra tech. This battle is no tech."

Xochitl marches forward with a stun blade.
"Not me though. I'm ready to get in the fray!"

The Harvesters stand ready with their cyberware, bats and stun knives. Lacuna tells me to sense the movement energy of the incoming Cloaks. A few blocks down, I feel the tech energy of several cars coming. I glance back at Lacuna. She smiles at my growth. She senses that there is no secret tech in the cars. She raises her hand to give us the all clear. Machado and Ramirez raise their hands. The Harvesters cheer.

As they do, the Cloaks drive up in tinted black cars. Several Cloak gang members empty out of the cars. They are donned in their gang outfit of black trench coats and shades. They file out with all manner of stun akrafenas (Ghanaian swords). The Cloaks raise them in a challenging stance. Out of the most luxurious black and gold car, steps a tall and fit dark skin woman with a huge afro. Sister Solace, the leader of the Cloaks, takes off her shades and faces Machado with one of her twin akrafena blades at the ready.

Sister Solace announces her intentions to every Harvester.
"Machado! You think you can harvest from me unnoticed?!"
Machado smirks at her challenge.
"Now, would I really be the one to do that? You always thought I was too loud anyways."
She ignores his jeers.
"If this was Kumasi, I'd have your head but we're going to have to settle this with a rumble. Can't have Gifty and her MPs now can we?" You win; I accept the loss of gear. I win, I get my gear back and some credits for the trouble."

He rubs his beard stubble.

"Sounds like a fair bargain, Solace. Harvesters; weapons up!"

The Harvesters brandish their weapons and cyberware.

Sister Solace yells at her own gang.

"Cloaks rise!"

Several Cloaks turn on their vibro-blades for the fray. The golden glow of them indicates their stun setting. With a wave of Solace's hand, the Cloaks rush the Harvesters. Pandemonium ensues. Sister Solace makes her way through the harvesters with her long akrafenas. Machado stays back issuing commands. Meanwhile Ramirez, Greene and Xochitl fight their way into the rumble. Xochitl's stun-blade locks with the Cloaks swords. Greene uses a metal pipe to his advantage. Ramirez on the other hand, swings her arm blade implants to duel. Lacuna and I are further behind Machado watching for tech amongst the chaos. Sister Solace reaches Machado who duels her with his arm blade. A circle forms around them while both gangs watch their leaders fracas. Sister Solace gains the upper hand with several parries and aggressive thrusts that put Machado on the defense. However, he feints and sweeps her leg. It catches her off guard. He rises to press his opening. When he does, a Cloak member pulls out a small blaster pistol to aim at him. Lacuna sees it. Before she can act, I send a shock to the pistol and its owner. Both gangs pause to stare at me. Then they look back at the site of the shock. The Cloak member's pistol tumbles out of his grip. Lacuna approves of my skill in pleasant surprise. Sister Solace glares at the gun-wielding Cloak and stabs him in the chest. She tells her other members to dispose of him.

Next, she addresses me.

"Damn shame the Harvesters found you first girl. It would be nice to have some Surge on my side. Lacuna it seems like you found your protégé, the next Voidess."

Lacuna laughs and places a hand on my shoulder. I wonder about Sister Solace's ideas.

Afterwards, she confronts Machado and Ramirez. *"Machado I'm letting this slide because one of my men broke the no tech rules. Plus, I didn't know you had new Surge members. That's just too much Surge for me. Anyways, good seeing you Voidess. Ramirez, take care of your brother; he needs to work on his offense.*
I trust I won't be seeing any Harvesters anytime soon.
Machado agrees with her.
"We're good right now."
She threatens him from getting any ideas.
"Keep it that way if you want to keep your numbers up."

She elegantly walks back to the black and gold car. The rest of the Cloaks join her in their cars and speed away. After a moment, the Harvesters spring into action.

Machado demands Greene update him. .
"Greene! Give me a damage report."
Greene studies his holopad.
"I think we hurt them more than they hurt us. Still, we got about thirty or so hurt pretty bad. Sister Solace handled about fifteen of our gang by herself!"
Ramirez sits in admiration.
"That lady never ceases to amaze me. And how about that shock? Afia, I had no idea you had it in you."
I stay humble.
"It was nothing. I have to protect Machado. I'm a Harvester now"
Lacuna agrees with my statement.

"Oui. That's a faster response than me. Well-done Afia. Sister Solace is not one to take broken rules lightly. She usually would have noticed that blaster pistol just as fast."

Machado reflects on that.

"I just hope she gets her affairs in order. Otherwise, she's going to have a mutiny on her hands. Anyways, let's go debrief."

End Chapter 6

****

Chapter 7

A month goes by while I work with the Harvesters. I acclimate well to Harvester culture. I even contemplate putting in some cyber implants in my body. I continue to train on my Surge with Lacuna. Furthermore, I'm dating Ramirez. Thus, I am a full-fledged Harvester now. I join the rest of the gang on several simple missions. None of the missions involve the Cloaks, but we do deal with the other gangs often.

Xochitl informs Machado that The Omnipotent One, the leader of the Techno Kids, wants to meet. The Omnipotent One is a pretentious, well-dressed person with a flair for opulence. They are light-skinned and with very low cut white hair. Their gang, the Techno Kids, trade in the illegal drug, Zela. The Omnipotent One uses several drug warehouses and often throws extravagant parties with Zela-infused palm wine. Machado decides to bring the main group of Harvesters together. Xochitl locates the message from the Omnipotent One. She layouts the message and then the plan on a large monitor.

Xochitl addresses us.
"Alright Harvesters, here is the plan from the Omnipotent One. Seems like a simple deal. He's offering up a bunch of smuggled gear from Kenya. We offer up cash and we're good to go. One caveat though. We're doing it in Sirius territory."

Xochitl outlines the location on the monitor. There are several pieces of tech outlining the location. It is within the labyrinth alleyways near the Sirius headquarters. The Sirius gang is known for its interconnectivity through a neural network, known as the Constellation. They work often as one and each have eye implants to fully immerse themselves. Due to their extensive training, it is rare that anyone leaves the Constellation. When they do, Sirius attempts to hunt them down. Still, some manage well on their own. Ramirez scrutinizes the area outlined on the monitor.

Ramirez slams the briefing room table.
"Diablo! You know that won't work. Sirius has too many eyes."
Xochitl responds to her concern.
"About that. The Omnipotent One has it covered. Ex-Sirius members. They can get us out as well. I just worry about Gifty and her military police. No Sirius protection means they can hack a channel."
Machado guesses it may be difficult.
"So we've got two caveats then."
Xochitl realizes the depth of the situation.
"Pinche. You're right. So what do we think?"
Greene states that the gear is too good to pass up.
"This could be risky. We're ok now, but imported gear. That could be really great."
Ramirez disagrees with the whole plan.
"Hermano, I don't like this one bit. I'll have to deal with Gifty most likely."
I ask about Gifty.
"Who's Gifty?"
Lacuna chimes in.
"You're better off not knowing. Now, ma souer, you know we can read tech readouts and hell we got Xochitl.

Xochitl bows in honor.

I add my skills to our mission as well.
"And you have me. I can support Lacuna. With the two of us you have enough Surge to handle anything."
Machado thinks about it.
"Si, pero we still have to keep you a bit under wraps. The Central Detective Agency is aware of more Surge activity in

the city. Not until I know you can handle your own. Lacuna they'll never take, but you are still young."

I sit back in frustration.

Lacuna leans over to me.
"It's for the best, D'accord?"

I'm still not happy. But I'm glad to at least be able to go on the journey.

End Chapter 7

****

<u>Chapter 8</u>

We park Xochitl's hovercar in a secluded spot near Sirius territory. Xochitl places a cloak on her hovercar. She outlines a location on her holopad and signals everyone to put on their frequencies. Machado grabs the bag of money for the deal. Lacuna notices several rainbow flags in Techno Kid colors. Ramirez holds up a fist and takes the lead. We follow the flags to a secluded area. There the Omnipotent One waits with their main bosses: Abdul and Nana. The Omnipotent One is tall, slender and wears a white robe lined with kente cloth. They often wear a hat on their head to match that is square and tilted to the side. Abdul is a thin bronze-skinned man with dark, short, and wavy hair. He also wears earrings. Nana is a tall dark-skinned, well-built bald man. The two enforce and handle almost all the Techno Kids' drug trade. Xochitl puts a firewall to the corners of the area. She hopes it will help block Sirius signals. There are no cameras surrounding us. The deal appears safe.

The Omnipotent One glides over to us.
"Machado and the women. Ramirez, Lacuna, Xochitl and Greene."
Greene is upset.
"For the hundredth time I'm not..."
They put up one of their hands.
"Please, hon. We know how you used to moonlight. Right?'
Greene concurs with their assessment.
"True, true. Though I think I prefer myself more masc-presenting."
They shrug about the whole ordeal.
"Whatever makes you happiest. Now onto the real business. O wait, I was so distracted with Greene and his charms that I didn't recognize you. Who is this lovely lady?"

They greet me. I cock an eyebrow. I wonder what they want from me.

I introduce myself.
"I'm Afia. Newer recruit, but great tracking skills. Pleased to meet you."
Ramirez stamps her feet.
"Enough Omni! Let's do this deal and go. Bad enough we're in Sirius territory."
Machado brings the bag to the Omnipotent One.
"Bien o no?"

They snap with their fingers. Nana comes forward with two duffel bags of imported Kenyan cyberware. When Machado opens one of the bags, our location floods with light and a voice on the loudspeaker calls out.

A gruff voice speaks.
"This is the military police. You are in violation of...O I see you are all going to run."

All hell breaks loose. We all scatter in every direction. The voice on the loudspeaker tells the military police to follow them. The owner of the voice is Gifty Amoah. The leader of the military police. A tall, thick and muscular dark-skinned woman with bantu knots. She is a highly skilled fighter who knows how to deal with Surge users. Furthermore, she keeps the gangs of Tesano in line from the other areas of Accra.

In the confusion, Abdul, Lacuna, Ramirez and Xochitl go in one direction. Machado, Nana, Greene, the Omnipotent One and I go in the other. Ramirez's group moves quickly from the military police by following Abdul's Techno Kid markers. Our group searches for the rainbow tags. However, we become lost. The military police close-in on us until a Sirius siren goes off elsewhere. A hooded figure drops down from the rooftops to greet us.

They speak to us.
"Greetings distinguished guests. I am Jiang. Omnipotent One, it was me who you contacted."

They take off their hood. An androgynous person with porcelain skin and protruding eyes is revealed. They are sporting a crew cut and shaved sides for their hair. The Omnipotent One recognizes them. They beckon us to follow them. We navigate the maze easily until we reach two Sirius guards. Jiang puts a hand up to pause us.

They whisper softly to not cause awareness.
"Hold. They will sense us through the communications."
Nana demands action.
"Why don't we just take them out?"
They put that idea to rest.
"Too risky. They're on a neural network. Remember? Someone will come fast."

Greene peers past the guards and sees military police lights not too far.

He gets the attention of us.
"Whatever we do needs to be fast. MPs on the horizon."
The Omnipotent One approaches me.
"New woman. What can you make of this? Can you help?"

I look at Machado for what to do next. He closes his eyes and shakes his head. Greene encourages me. The Omnipotent One and Nana stare at me in deep concern. After weighing my decisions, I send a Surge spark. It silently damages the neural network of both guards. Greene gives a little cheer. The Omnipotent One becomes delighted at my display. Jiang expresses surprise by the appearance of Surge. Machado reprimands me.

He warns me to not use the Surge often.
"Conyo! What did I say?! In Sirius territory as well. "
I stand up to him.
"We had no choice!"
He barks at me.
"We would've figured it out!"
Jiang stops both of us.
"Hey there? Are you two done? We need to hurry up and get out of this region now. The MPs and Sirius will be swarming soon.

We move rapidly after the update. Jiang guides us to the end of Sirius territory. They bow in respect. We return the gesture in good faith. As we leave Sirius territory, they contact someone on their frequency.

They amplify their frequency.
"Chyou, did you see that Surge? That's not a CDA move. Too precise."
Chyou scans Jiang's eye data. Then she replies in a calculating manner.
"Yes, sib. This can clear us of the Constellation once and for all. Everyone thought the Voidess was the prize. Seems this new lady Afia will be good enough."
They hesitate.
"You sure? She's pretty young. Can't we go about the Constellation in a different way? We're really about to give up this woman to Sirius?"
She cuts into her frequency.
"Yes Jiang! It's either them or us. Remember we matter most. After this, you can tell me your ideas for Lily Cheung. And remember, call me Daiyu now!"

She shuts off her frequency after. Jiang sighs. They wonder if attacking the Constellation of Sirius head on would be better. They prefer bombing network links and Sirius politicians, like Lily Cheung. They think Sirius will contact the Harvesters soon. But, they also create a backup plan in case the Surge user trade doesn't work.

End Chapter 8

****

<u>Chapter 9</u>

A month later in the neutral bar, Rick's Cafe.

　　If there's a bright spot in the Tesano municipality, it's Rick's Cafe. The bar is a great source of information and safety all while grabbing a drink. At Rick's all gangs are welcome. Even the Central Detective Agency (CDA) is welcome. Rick keeps weapons locked, security turrets on and some of the best Jamaican food in Accra. At least, most Ghanaians believe he's Jamaican. No one really knows where in the Caribbean he is from. We enter for some new information and some drinks. All the gang and CDA present watch us for a moment. Ramirez steps up and glares at the crowd. Everyone goes back to their business. Rick waves us over.

　　Rick cautions us to behave.
"Welcome Harvesters. No fighting now ya' hear? I know about ya' rumble."
　　Xochitl walks up and admires Rick's turrets.
"Hola Rick! One of these days, you're going to have to let me check out those babies."
　　He mocks her.
"'Ey Xochitl. Ya' going to work as me mechanic 'den? Machado and the Harvesters not paying enough?"
　　Ramirez shuts down his jokes.
"Screw you Rick. She's getting paid just fine."
　　He raises his voice with excitement. *"Ramirez! Lacuna the Voidess! Machado! Good to see you. And who is this new one here?"*
　　I greet him heartily.
"My name is Afia. Nice to meet you Rick."
　　He chuckles with mirth.

"Manners on the gyal? Good good, well the Harvesters are a pretty good crew, but let me know if you ever want some other work."

Machado greets him then tells us information.
"Hola Rick. Hey crew, I need to grab some info on a deal. I'll be back in a moment."

Ramirez furrows her brow and asks.
"Need backup? Hermano, we got you."

He replies to her concern.
"No, hermana. And don't give me that face. I'm at Rick's, you know I'll be safe."

He walks over to a group of Sirius gang members. He picks out one of the members. A gang member lady, with the signature Sirius cybernetic data-searching eyes, analyzes him.

Sirius speaks to him.
"Welcome Machado. I trust you received our frequency message."

He acknowledges the Sirius members.
"Yes I did. Guess it was only a matter of time before one of your cameras picked up that display of Surge. I want the Harvesters to be clean of this. Also I can't give this up for free."

The Sirius members search their database for guidance. Machado watches all the members' eyes glow and hum with activity.

One of the Sirius members gives an answer.
"We know of a military shipment heading out from a train yard in Lome. It's got plenty of tech and cyber implants. You can keep the tech or sell it to us for profit. Your choice. Note that this shipment is likely more than you've ever pulled. It will

finally be enough to truly help your homeland. You could even fight the military."

Machado rubs his fingers through his hair.
"This is very promising. However, it's a lot to give up one of those ladies. They trust me. This is big for my blood family, but for my Harvester family it's a dangerous move."

A Sirius member leans back.
"The choice is yours Machado. If you don't go with this, then we expose you and you get nothing for it. Gifty and her MPs will be on you like flies. You and your sister will be deported. And the Harvesters will be no more. What will it be?"

He offers a counteroffer.
"How about you take Lacuna the Voidess instead? You've surely heard of the Voidess's power? I just feel really guilty giving up the young one. For mi hermana's sake."

Another Sirius member continues the thought process.
"That may be possible, but the young Surge woman, Afia, is it? Is far more malleable than the Voidess. Still, the Voidess is skilled, and she never did join the Central Detective Agency. Again, the choice is yours. Either way earns benefits and consequences."

Machado gets up.
"Fair enough. How should I get Lacuna for you?"

Sirius finishes their statements.
"There will be one of us on the Lome shipment. Once the trade is made, we will erase all footage in real time."

Across the cafe, I grab a seat at the bar. I order a refreshing Club beer. Some members of a gang called the Old Guard, question me. The Old Guard is a gang who often use explosives and military ordinance. They often drape themselves in a debonair steampunk style. They tend to be territorial and don't trust average citizens at all.

A drunk, yet formal Old Guard member, stares at me.

"Why are you sitting here in Rick's Cafe? Are you a new dancer from the Legon streets?"

I quizzically ask him.

"What are you talking about? I'm a Harvester."

The other more composed Old Guard member states.

"You don't have any implants, you're no Harvester. The only civilians that come in here are businessmen or prostitutes. As you are not a man with money, that makes you a prostitute."

I stand up from my barstool.

"Really now!? I'm not going to take this talk from you!"

I punch the second Old Guard member. He falls over a table. The drunken Old Guard squares up to fight. However, Ramirez smacks a bottle on his head before they can do anything. The rest of the Old Guard members in the bar stare at us. I ready my Surge power for the fight. Lacuna shuts off my Surge flow from across the bar. I peer at her in surprise.

I shout at her.

"Lacuna? How in the hell?"

While I focus on Lacuna, the first Old Guard lunges at me. Ramirez steps in front of me. She sends the Old Guard member crashing down with a powerful blow. The rest of the Old Guard rushes us. Some of the other gangs harangue us to fight. Before the fight worsens, Rick fires a vibro-rifle in the air.

He yells at me.

"Gyal! You just got here and you're already starting a mess!"

I try to explain.

"But these guys just…"

He stops me from speaking.

"Nah' want to hear it. 'Dems the Old Guard. They have rules that are older than the Surge. You lost your bar privileges for the day. And you too Ramirez. Old Guard, take your two bums

out. And the rest of ya' anymore nonsense and you're not in here for a week!"

Xochitl sighs at the madness of the situation.
"Pinche Ramirez! You're always ruining a good drink."

Lacuna calls Machado.
"Machado! It's time for us to go. Hope you got what you needed."

He joins us at the bar and we walk out.

I complain about the gang fight.
"Those Old Guard people sucked."

Ramirez laughs at my stress.
"Pay them no mind. They don't do much but whine and wear fancy clothes. Still, when you need explosives, they're the best. Unfortunately, we can't kill them."

Xochitl rolls her eyes.
"So, it wasn't just Ramirez who ruined my drink?! You ruin drinks too?"

Lacuna plays peacekeeper.
"Zut. You'll be fine Afia. We'll go back to Rick's and learn about the Old Guard another day. What did you learn from Sirius Machado?"

He shows the data from his holopad.
"Military transport out of Lome. Best haul ever. Sirius says it will be great."

Ramirez wonders about us going to Tome.
"Hermano, do we mess with the Togon military? That's new territory."

He persists on us taking the job.
"We do when the score is this big. It will make us strong enough to help our people back home hermana. Then we can keep the military or anyone off of our backs."

Xochitl agrees to the job.

"Bueno. It sounds like a lot of good supplies and tech. I'm game if Sirius gives me security details."

Machado concludes our discussion.

"Let's go back and tell Greene. Then we can prepare. He'll hold down the fort, I'm sure."

End Chapter 9

****

Chapter 10

Lome Military train yard.

Our Harvester team of Machado, Lacuna, Xochitl, Ramirez and I head out to the train yard in Lome, Togo. Machado orders the team on several tasks.

He asks for Xochitl's advice.
"Xochitl. Do you think we can get to the supply train before it leaves?"
She laughs at his suggestion.
"No mamas wey. Sirius only gave us security information. Even if we know which train car it is, we'll have to disconnect it from the engine car. Splitting off at Keta Lagoon is our best bet. It's small enough for the transport to hover over. So everyone hops out with the loot."
He notes her strategy.
"Alright, Lacuna, Surge whatever security electronics you can. Afia, locate any tech on the guards. Ramirez, cover Afia. I'll go with Lacuna. Xochitl, you already know what to do."
She heads to her hovercar.
"Bueno! Lacuna just make sure you send a pulse before we hit that checkpoint. The Togon military will be on us if you don't. See you all at the new harvest of cyber gear!"
Lacuna claps back.
"Bonne chance, Xochitl, I'll be fine. Afia, the checkpoint may be too complex for you. So, when I need to emit the pulse, you'll have to check for the train security.
I nod my head in affirmation.
"I got your back Lacuna. With all your training, I'm sure I can handle that."

While we prepare ourselves, Machado secretly contacts Sirius that we're on the train. Ramirez and I enter the back of the supply train. We scan the cars for supplies and guards.

Meanwhile, Lacuna and Machado journey to the engine car. Their goal is to set up our exit after we obtain the stolen goods. Lacuna sends a wave of Surge to short circuit several security turrets. Due to her skill the wave is too subtle to show up on any military censors. This is also due to the supply train traveling on a magnetic railroad. In the back of the train, Ramirez and I subdue guards while hacking through each train car. I move ahead. Ramirez trails behind to shut off military frequencies. We find the first supply car of military cyber gear. We send frequencies to everyone. The next phase of the plan begins. Machado and Lacuna reach the engine car and hold up the conductor. They keep the train on its path towards Keta Lagoon. After restraining the conductor, Machado leads Lacuna towards the other military supply car. When they arrive, a member of Sirius is waiting.

Lacuna remarks at the Sirius member.
"What in the hell is Sirius doing here?! What the hell is this?!"

Machado quickly places a Surge dampener on her from behind.

She rages against him.
"Machado, what are you doing?! What is the meaning of this?" She pauses for a moment then realizes her own set up. *"Wait you made a deal over me. Machado how could you?! After all we've been through. And dampeners? Really?! "*
He fights back tears.
"It was you or Afia. Sirius made us on that bad Techno Kid deal. Afia would be taken from us. The Harvesters disbanded and Ramirez and I'd be deported. Instead, Afia is ok and I can finally help my family. Figure you'd accept yourself over Afia."
The Sirius member interrupts.

"Thank you Machado for your payment. We will take good care of the Voidess. We are clearing the video evidence as we speak."

The Sirius member shows the erasure on their holopad.

Machado ponders something on his mind.
"Bien. But, what will you do to her? Don't you dare hurt her. I know we're square but still. "
The Sirius member gloats.
"Of course not. We won't harm her. Our goal is to hand her to the military. They will decide what to do with her"
Machado scowls and prepares his cyber arm blade.
"Damn, you Sirius! You're as shifty as ever. This wasn't part of the deal." Machado steps toward the Sirius member.
The Sirius member stretches out a nanowire.
"I wouldn't move if I were you. I can use this nanowire to hack into those implants of yours."
Lacuna yells at both of them.
"Merde, this dampener! Come on Machado. You know Sirius wouldn't play this straight. You're a fool for believing that."
He tries to speak.
"I...I can fix this."

The Sirius member eyes both Lacuna and Machado.

Lacuna shakes her head.
"Too late for that. I will not be a slave to be experimented on by the military again. You both can let me out or I will figure this out for myself."
Xochitl chirps in through the frequency. She comments on our train's progress and the mission.
"Checkpoint coming up Lacuna. Hit the pulse."
The Sirius member states there is no issue.

"There's nothing you can do. Those are improved Surge dampeners. Don't worry about the checkpoint. We'll pass it by it no problem."

Machado makes a move toward the Sirius member with his arm blade. The Sirius member shoots the nanowire at the blade and hacks Machado's implants. Lacuna concentrates to gather her Surge force.

She reaches out to me telepathically.
<Afia, lend me your Surge. There's so much more I wish I could've told you. Don't lose faith in yourself. I will always be there to guide you through the trials ahead. Adore ma souer>
I reply and try to figure out what is going on.
<Lacuna, how are you doing this? Wait, what do you mean so much more?! Why are you saying this?!>
Suddenly, my Surge flares up and out of me. I fall to my knees. Ramirez rushes over.

She asks me what I'm feeling.
"Afia, are you ok babe? What's going on? You're shaking."

She watches as the Surge continuously flows from me. The Surge travels to the other supply car. In the other car, Lacuna glows blue with Surge.

The Sirius member does not know what to make of everything changing.
"But the dampener? How can your Surge still work?"

Lacuna opens her eyes. They shimmer like blue sapphires. Her whole-body floats while she glows blue.

She expresses everything that she is.
"I am more powerful than you could imagine. I will not be kept as a military slave. This is the only way to break free. So,

fuck you Sirius and fuck you Machado for thinking this would work."

She draws in a great amount of Surge from me and any tech in the train. Then the Surge buildup in her implodes, taking Machado, the Sirius member, and the whole train car with her. Pieces of other cars go flying into the lagoon. A burst of Surge erupts from me. I am blown back into Ramirez. The engine speeds through the checkpoint with no EMP pulse. The checkpoint signals flash warning signs to alert the Togon military of intruders. The other supply car stalls without the engine car. Xochitl's hovercar speeds over to where our supply car is. We quickly enter her hovercar to avoid detection.

Xochitl yells about the outcome.
"Chinga! What on earth just happened?!Where's Machado and Lacuna?! The rest of the train, the gear?"

Ramirez studies me. I'm too in shock to respond. She probably thinks that this destruction is because of my powers. I notice her scrutiny.

I plead with her to understand me.
"Ramirez? This wasn't me honey. This was Lacuna. At least I think it was..."
She pushes me away.
"Get away from me you monster! Conyo, Xochitl, get us out of here fast! And I hope next time we have better intel!"
Xochitl pauses our altercation.
"Hey I don't know what happened either. And what about all the gear? Machado? Lacuna?"
Ramirez slams her fist down.
"Diablo puta! I said just go. I can't speak about it right now. We need to leave before the Togon military comes."

Military helicopters close in on the chaotic scene. Ramirez sits in the back of the transport in sadness and anger. Tears stream down her face. I sit in the front mourning Lacuna. However, I am also wary of Ramirez. Xochitl witnesses the exchange between us. She is apprehensive of both of us. She turns the radar-jamming tech on in the hovercar. The hovercar races away from the train in silence.

End Chapter 10

****

Chapter 11

Back at the Harvesters' headquarters.

Ramirez storms into the headquarters. She breezes by everyone. Xochitl and I enter the headquarters with trepidation. Greene attempts to stop one of us for information.

He asks in confusion.
"Will someone tell me what happened? Ladies, where's the cyber implants and the gear? Where's Machado!? Lacuna!? Y'all frequencies haven't been on in ages."
Ramirez yells at him to shut up.
"Can it Greene! We'll talk later, I need a moment to myself."

She enters Machado's private room and slams the door.

Greene talks to Xochitl and I again.
"Afia or Xochitl? Could you please update me?!"
Xochitl conveys what is going.
"It's bad Greene. There was a huge Surge implosion in the supply car. I think it took out Lacuna, Machado and the gear. Ramirez swears it was Afia. I don't know. I don't think Afia's got power like that."
I blurt out my feelings.
"It's impossible for me. It had to be Lacuna. I'm not sure how she did it. Or why, but it wasn't me. Ramirez isn't hearing it though."
Greene acknowledges my explanation.
"Well that means Ramirez is in charge for now. We needed that gear shipment. We're going to have to raid another Cloak warehouse."
I beg Xochitl to see me positively.
"Hey Xochitl, you believe me right? I couldn't have done that. No way it was me."
She shrugs at my perspective.

"I guess so Afia. We'll see what Ramirez says."

In Machado's room, Ramirez sits with furious tears. She realizes a frequency buzz is coming through Machado's holopad. It's the Sirius gang. She puts the frequency through.

Sirius starts their demands.
"Ms. Ramirez. You need to provide what your brother could not. Your brother made a deal to erase all traces of Harvester Surge activity in exchange for Lacuna."
She asks for more details.
"There's no way he would do that. What footage? What deal?"
Sirius continues to tell her what she wants to know.
"The footage from your deal gone wrong with the Techno Kids. Afia Osuwu used her Surge powers. Gifty Amoah and her MPs would be very interested in that footage."
She sits back in her seat.
"Damn. What do you need from me then? What happens next?"
Sirius answers with their request.
"We need the Surge candidate, Afia. Lacuna would have smoothed everything over. Now we have no choice."
She attempts to not give them a chance of any Surge candidate.
"And if I refuse?
Sirius explains the consequences.
"Well, then you'll be deported, and the Harvesters disbanded. Also, we will make this worse. You won't ever be able to support your family in the Dominican Republic again."

She pauses and reflects. She weighs her options.

She counters with some questions.

"Bueno. What happens to Afia if I give her to you? Does that make everything good? Because I lost gear and people too.

Sirius deduces that it may not go the way she wants.

"That is the military's decision. But either way you need to figure it out. If not, all of Accra will destroy the Harvesters."

She decides on a plan.

"Hmmm. I have on an idea. It will take some time. I'll patch you on this frequency when Afia's ready for you."

Sirius ends the meeting.

"Sirius awaits your call."

Ramirez contacts Sister Solace on her frequency.

She groans at seeing Ramirez.

"What the hell do you want? Was that train implosion you?"

Ramirez does not hesitate and immediately denies it.

"No, it wasn't. But I got a deal for you. Betting big with our last cash. We didn't get the gear we needed. So I'll need your finest gear. We'll come to you."

Sister Solace is skeptical.

"O? If you fuck up, you'll be surrounded. That's fair. How much do you want?"

Ramirez states her price.

"All of it then a 30% cut."

Sister Solace raises her brow.

"30%? Are you mad?"

Ramirez ups the ante.

"40%. We'll do the selling and I have a little bonus for you."

Sister Solace gives in.

"Fine. Going under your brother huh? Always thought you were a better leader. Lacuna cool with it?"

Ramirez calms her.

"Yeah yeah. Everything is fine. Don't worry you'll like the bonus. And keep this between us.

She reminds Ramirez.

"Hey, you know when and where to meet right? Same as usual. And again, don't bullshit me Ramirez."

Ramirez smiles at her

"Todo bien baby."

Next, Ramirez contacts Gifty.

Ramirez talks quickly.
"Hey asshole, got a hot tip for you."

Gifty responds with confusion.
"And? What do you want?"

Ramirez says the details of her recent deal with Sirius and the Cloaks. .
"Deal between Sirius and Cloaks. Harvesters will be there too. I want immunity for us."

Gifty mulls over her idea.
"What goods will they have?"

Ramirez says more to get her attention. .
"Military grade cyberware."

This prompts Gifty to agree on the deal. .
"Military grade? Why didn't you say so? You won't get a cut on this. What's in it for you?"

Ramirez settles Gifty's mind.
"Don't worry about it. Just give us immunity."

Gifty signs off of Ramirez's frequency. Ramirez analyzes her notes. She prepares a speech for the Harvesters. She tells us to gather in the main hall.

She lays out her plan.
"Alright Harvesters, as much as it pains me to say it, I'm in charge of this racket right now. Both Machado and Lacuna have been lost to us during an accident. It was a mission gone awry. I'll let you know more later."

The Harvesters murmur amongst each other. Ramirez cuts a slight glance at me then Xochitl. I back away from the crowd. I thought Xochitl was clear, but perhaps Ramirez wants no opposition. Xochitl shifts focus between Ramirez and me. She has uncertainty about the situation. Ramirez puts a fist up to stop the chatter. She continues her speech.

She calls out to Greene.
"Greene, get me some solid Harvesters. We're going to hit the main Cloak warehouse quick and silent. The Cloaks will come after us. However, with Afia and Xochitl we should be able to slip in and out. It's not military-grade gear like we tried for in Lome. However, we need the resources."

Greene gathers a few Harvesters and prepares for Ramirez's mission. I go up to her.

I ask about her suspicion.
"What was that look for? Why are you like this? You know I'm still trustworthy honey."
She moves away from me.
"Afia, don't honey me. Still, I need your help for this mission. So at least we can work together. Xochitl you in?"
She cautiously agrees.
"Guess so. Can we take some backup? It's not the same without Machado and Lacuna."
Ramirez calms her down.
"Hey, remember Greene will gather the best and the brightest. He will have to be here at headquarters in the meantime though. The Cloaks still think we're dealing with the train issue. So come on, let's go to the warehouse now."

Ramirez heads out and types a couple messages in her frequency. I sense the strange coding of the messages. Before I can react, Xochitl calls me over. We ready ourselves for the Cloaks warehouse.

End Chapter 11
****

Chapter 12

We arrive at the Cloaks warehouse. Ramirez orders us to set-up positions. She also dials her frequency to prepare Sirius, Gifty and Sister Solace for their respective meetings. The warehouse is eerily quiet with no lights or activity. We are all tense from our last mission. As such, something feels off, I'm just not sure what.

Ramirez urges me on.
"Alright Afia, hack the first door so we can get it in. Hey Greene, we're headed in."

She contacts Gifty first.

Gifty reads Ramirez loud and clear.
"Copy, Ramirez."

I scan the door. When I do, I send an uncontrolled burst hack throughout the building that opens all of the doors. My powers are becoming harder to control. I wonder if it's grief for Lacuna or if this is how the Surge transforms. I eye Ramirez nervously after my mistake. She sighs.

She explains to the Harvesters.
"Slight security problem everyone. All the warehouse doors are open. So we're going to have to move a lot more quickly. You two Harvesters help Xochitl and Afia load up the main cyber implants from the storage room. I'm going with this guy to get the special gear."

She heads upstairs to an unguarded room with cyber implants. She sees several newer cyberware implants promised by Sister Solace. Her Harvester assistant collects the goods.

She calls into the Sirius frequency.

"Alright Sirius, if you want to come get the girl she's here at the main warehouse now."
Sirius explains themselves.
"We have sent notice to the military of our deal. They will arrive to collect everything and everyone. Interestingly, the military has paid a lower sum than usual. We hope you haven't tried anything stupid like your brother. Once we have Afia, all your debts will be paid."

The other Harvester looks quizzically at Ramirez. Before he can say anything, she shoots an arm blade into his head. She grabs the gear and turns on one of the main warehouse lights. This signals Sister Solace. The other Harvesters, Xochitl, and I freeze when the light comes on. One by one the warehouse lights turn on. We follow the lights to a waiting Sister Solace and her gang of Cloaks. They stand above us on a walkway. With the distraction, Ramirez exits the warehouse.

Sister Solace applauds our efforts.
"Well, well. Welcome Harvesters and Afia, was it? You down to try a new gang because the old one sold you out."
I talk to my side.
"Xochitl, what is she talking about?"
She throws her hands up.
"Yo no se!" She speaks to Solace. *"Hey puta, where's Ramirez!?"*
Sister Solace casually walks over.
"I have no idea. She made a deal and said there was a bonus. Guess you two are the bonus. Shit, I don't need any cut after this."

Xochitl and I exchange glances.

Sister Solace continues her theatrics.

"Why the long faces? Yes, your friend sold you out. Who knew Machado would have the mutiny and not me.

Xochitl cuts her short.
"Machado is dead. You're lying about Ramirez. This was a usual heist."

Solace shrugs at what Xochitl tells her.
"Hmm that might explain where Lacuna is. Still, whether you believe it or not, it's no matter. Cloaks, disable the Surge candidate and the tech woman, kill the rest."

The Harvesters break out their cyber implants and fire pulses at the Cloaks. The Cloaks answer the pulses with vibro-gun blasts. I send up my Surge to deflect the blasts. I lose control of my power again. This time I inadvertently lock all the firing weapons in the warehouse. Everyone looks surprised. Suddenly, military police sirens wail nearby.

A Cloak member rushes to Sister Solace.
"Boss, it's Gifty and her MPs. They're coming to us fast. What do we do?!"

She kicks out in anger.
"That bitch Ramirez." She makes the connection with the MPs and no Ramirez. *"Shit, she double-crossed us!. Cloaks get your swords ready!"*

Several members of the Cloaks unsheathe their swords.

I grab Xochitl by the shoulder.
"Xochitl, we gotta go. This is way too hot. We have to get back to your hovercar."

Gifty and her MPs bust into the warehouse. Both Harvesters and Cloaks fight them. Sister Solace fends off some of the military as they swarm in. Xochitl and I exit the warehouse but can't find the hovercar.

Xochitl searches frantically for hovercar.
"Dammit Ramirez! She must have taken it. Where are we going to go? What are we going to do!? I got it. We'll have to hack a car. C'mon, Afia!"

She screams as a Cloak stabs me in the lower back. My lower back sears with pain. Blood gushes as the energy leaks from my body. Xochitl slashes the Cloak dead with her machete. I slump down to the floor.

Xochitl remains frantic.
"Afia don't worry. We'll get you patched up. Come on puta! This place is in chaos. Greene can help us."

A car across the street starts up. Xochitl traces the engine start to my outstretched hand.

I think and lightly say.
"Funny how much control I have when I'm dying."
Xochitl angrily tells me to stop lying.
"You're not dying on me Afia. Let me help."
Military troops and MPs gather closer.

I gather Xochitl close.
"Xochitl, listen to me. You've got to get out of here. I'll just drag you down. We couldn't go back to the headquarters anyways. All of this was probably Ramirez's idea. Greene won't trust us. Get out of here now Xochitl!"
She stammers before getting up.
"But...I...I'll come back for you Afia. I promise. I'll find help and I'll come back."

She gets in the car and speeds off to find help. I hear the military gunfire dying down. I listen to both gangs yelling at the military while being arrested. A military soldier walks up to me.

They recognize my injury.

"Major Abeem! Look, there's a civilian here. She needs help."

The major orders the soldier to do a scan.

"Give her a scan, what does she have on her?"

They read back the data.

"She's got no implants or tattoos. No Cloak scars either. She's not gang related. But oh! Ma'am, she has crazy amounts of Surge in her. Wonder how she got crossed up in this?"

Major Abeem ponders all the possibilities.

"Maybe she was part of a gang deal gone bad. She would've been a good weapon for the gangs. I'm sure the central detective agency would be happy to protect her." She then crouches down to my level. *"Hey there sweetie. The military is going to get this wound patched up in no time. The doctors will be happy to help with some meds. You've also got a lot of Surge in you. That means I'm sure the central detective agency can help with the health insurance."*

I groggily ask.

"Central detective agency? What? Who are you?"

She formally states.

"I'm Major Abeem of the Ghanian military down here in Accra. We sometimes support the MPs. As for The Central Detective Agency, they take in stray Surge people to help with their affairs. You are?"

I thank her.

"Afia. Thanks, Major Abeem."

She smiles at me.

"Please. You can call me Abeem.

End of Chapter 12 and Part 1

****

Files from the Desk of a Surge Detective - A History

The Central Detective Agency (CDA) is a military branch of Surge members who have vowed to help the military with their newfound powers. The detective agency formed three years after the Surge to give more control of the Surge to the military. Secondly, the CDA was used to reduce the number of Surge candidates who were experimented on by the military. Free of Surge dampeners and whatever military experiments the military uses, the CDA is free to live as relatively normal human beings. Occasionally, they are called slurs, like shockhead, for their powers. Still, most of the CDA is respected by civilians. Most of the time, they act independently of the military and don't always use similar procedures. While the CDA has only a few Surge candidates, they make up for it with their individual agents. One such agent is the young Afia Osuwu. The year is 2339, she is an ex-Harvester turned CDA. She explores disturbances primarily in Accra, Ghana. From time to time, she also has missions outside of Accra. Afia's files about her cases provide a backdrop of her experiences in a world after The Surge.

Chapter 13: Detective File 5 - Cloaked

After many months of training with the CDA, I am happy to be on my own. The head detective, Captain Yaa, is strict as hell. Still, her leadership remains invaluable to me. She is similar to Lacuna. Now, I use my powers to solve cases instead of smuggling cyberware. I find it strange to work for the military. It goes against everything the Harvesters are. Still, I admit it is safer for me and the benefits are nice. Like this new government apartment. It has all modern furniture and new appliances. The view is also lovely. Before I can relax, Captain Yaa connects to my frequency.

She greets me.
"Detective Afia, are you there?"
I confirm my presence.
"Yes Captain Yaa."
She asks how I am doing.
"I hope you like your new space."
I respond, while patting the fancy sofa.
"It's nice. The CDA lets you live comfortably."
She smiles at my comfort.
"Good to hear. Anyways, I have your first solo case. There's been a murder at the Stargazer Club. Might have been a patron there. The murder seems similar to another we've noticed in the area. I'll send you the file."
I imagine what type of club it is.
"Stargazer Club – it's a strip club/brothel, right? This will be a new experience for me. Hope Abeem is ok with this. Not exactly a good new case for someone with a girlfriend. "
She ignores my concern.
"Your lover will have to be fine. This is the nature of the work. Now remember, this is a solo case. I can only be used for research or CDA access matters. I'm sure you can figure out solutions for everything. Captain Yaa out."

I do not get a chance to ask for something else. Something that my girlfriend, Abeem, would be happy about instead. I debate whether or not to let Abeem know where the case is. I believe I'll let her know later, to avoid unwanted stress. I peruse the case file to find that the brothel is near Legon, the high roller entertainment district. A place where the upper-class gamble for more than they need. Many other places in Accra could benefit from the revenue instead of them. Anyways, I head outside with my CDA equipment to my government hovercar.

End Chapter 13

****

Chapter 14

I reach the Stargazer Club. I observe an evidence team scrutinize the crime scene. I flash my CDA badge to get in close. I Surge scan the dead body. The body belongs to one of the usual john or customers. I continue to scan him. I find a large wound from a sword. My initial hypothesis is that the attacker is a Cloak member. However, there appears to be no cauterization of the wound from a Cloak vibro-katana. I create a Surge recreation of the victim's last moments to be sure. I outline something cutting into the john. I note the strange stab wound in my holopad. Then I proceed to the Stargazer Club to question the patrons. A large bouncer stops me from entering.

They demand for my ID.
"Hey you got ID?"
I state that I'm a CDA detective.
"I'm CDA and I need to ask you a couple of questions about the victim over there."
They shrug and tell me nothing new.
"Like I told your evidence team. Dude comes walking over bleeding from that street. Happens after he goes out of the club."
I ask more questions.
"Did he come out with a girl?"
They shake their head.
"Nah, he probably got killed in the alleyway, but there's nothing over there. I checked."

I roll my eyes at the bouncer. I walk into the club to search for the mamasan or main owner of the joint. Strobe lights and pumping music pulses all around the club in spite of the murder outside. Strippers hang high from the ceilings on suspended bars. At center stage, an attractive femme and masc couple climb on hovering stripper poles. The lights in the club change multiple colors in tune with the sound of credits lighting up the strippers' wristbands. Also, submissive people dance half-naked in cages that move up and down vertically. I amble over to a tall stripper with wavy curls, who is head to toe in tattoos. I interrogate the stripper about her mamasan.

The stripper starts the conversation first.
"Hey, pretty woman. Care to enjoy a private show or do you wish to lie back on the couch right here? The name's Laila by the way. Also, I have a little something extra if that's your fancy."

She motions downward and spins in place. She is charming and even my type, but I remain an inquiring detective.

I surmise an idea to make this meaningful for both of us.
"Sure. I'll let you entertain me if you'll answer some questions.
Laila furrows her brows.
"O you must be CDA. What the hell do you need? Hurry up. Ask your questions then pay me."
I place my hand on my heart and fake being hurt.
"Damn. I like having fun while I work babe. But fine. First, any working ladies left here in the last few hours? And two, where is your mamasan?"
She promptly answers.
"Mamasan is upstairs. As for the other question, yeah we had a few girls leave. But because their shift ended. But I did see some dudes got aggressive as before they left."
I raise an eyebrow.
"Really now?"
Laila walks over to another patron to say hello. Then she comes back to me.

"Yeah, but once the bouncer came, the dudes left. That's when some girls who were actually on their shift left too. Ask the mamasan. Now, pay up oppressor."

I flinch at that rough moniker.

"Ugh, here you go."

I pay Laila. She performs a lap dance for another patron. Moments like these, I wish for my time in the Harvesters to return. Average citizens respect the CDA, but not the lower class and hustlers. I flash my CDA badge at more bouncers and go upstairs. I find the mamasan sitting at her desk. She wears a head wrap and a brightly colored sari. She takes a long drag from her cigarette.

She inquires about my presence.

"What do you want, CDA? Come to ask about the dead john outside? Serves him right for always harassing the girls with his crew. They probably did him in themselves. He kept getting his friends kicked out."

I take a seat in front of her.

"You think his crew did this? Did any of them have blades?"

She thinks about that.

"They all carried vibro-guns. The bouncer checked them at the door. Maybe they had blades hidden outside. But Legon isn't Tesano you know."

I laugh at her even reminding me of that.

"Of that I'm well aware."

She is nonplussed.

"Still, the random homeless person here could handle you in a bad alley."

I write down more on my holopad.

"I'll check that alley in a minute. Couple more questions. Where did your girls on shift go? Who were they?"

The mamasan puffs smoke from her cigarette.

"Most went to the casinos after their shift. I let some do extra hustling with the high rollers at Adinkras. Most of the ones on that shift were my plus-size ladies. They always do well with the high rollers. Dinae is the main attraction of them. The other two are new so I don't know them as well. Names are Bena and Kari I think. I'm sure you can figure it out."

I record everything she tells me. As I write, she tells me off.

"Will that be all, oppressor?"

I breathe heavily. Her snarky tone is annoying. When I leave, I tell her I'm set.

"Yes, that should be it."

End Chapter 14

****

Chapter 15: Detective File 5 - Cloaked

I make my way to the alley the bouncer mentioned. Using my Surge, I locate a vibro-gun shot in one of the walls. I remark that this looks like a scuffle. I know it is between the dead john and one of the girls. Before I leave, I examine the other wall more closely. There are traces of Surge in it. I theorize that one of the girls is a Surge candidate. Non- CDA and not me or Lacuna is a rarity. I file everything in my holopad. I drive to the casino area. While driving, Abeem calls me on my frequency.

She excitedly greets me.
"Hey hun. How you doing?"
I take a moment to admit where I am.
"Doing great. I got my first solo case and it led to a death near a strip club."
She raises her voice.
"A strip club?! Why didn't you tell me?!"
I try to soothe her oncoming anger.
"I didn't want your concern to interfere with my investigation. Don't worry, nothing happened. Check the cameras if you want."
She clears her throat.
"No need for that. You're a sneaky one Afia. Anyways, where to next?"
I tell her my next location.
"I'm headed to the casinos. I think Adinkras."
She sighs and knows my mission may be dangerous.
"I wish I could back you up. When will the CDA allow military escorts?"
I tell her.

She beams with happiness.

I produce a strange look.

She still gives me a word of caution.

I laugh it off.

I close out the frequency. I park my car at a rail station. Then I get on the rail to Adinkras, the largest casino in Ghana. Once there, I gaze at the huge Adinkra symbols adorning the entrance.

Adinkras: slot machines, holovid lottery, Senegalese wrestling bets, and even the cowrie shell games are all gambling vices here. Each gamble goes off with a myriad of lights and sounds. The slots and lottery are on the second floor where you enter from the rail. Big wrestling arena betting is on the third floor. Down on the first floor are cowrie shell and Bao games. However, patrons can also get all their drinks, drugs and women downstairs too. I descend to the first floor. The ceilings and walls illuminate with ever-changing colors and shapes. I freeze when I find a trace of Surge hovering in the air. I follow the Surge line to a trio of ladies. I see possibly Dinae, Bena and Kari. I prepare to explain myself. Before that happens, Bena senses my Surge trace as well. Bena and I lock eyes.

At that moment, I follow my protocol.

Kari and Dinae stare at me with whimsy. Meanwhile, Bena immediately runs away from me before I can finish. I chase after her. While running, she Surge blasts slot machines that release tokens everywhere. The tokens slow me down because several patrons rush to grab the tokens. Bena knocks through a few games of Bao, beads spilling everywhere. I dodge the ire of the players and almost catch up to Bena. Bena cuts up to the second floor and shoots a few sparks behind her. Several people duck the sparks in the casino. The casino guards come out of the security rooms to see what the commotion is. The guards almost stop me, but I quickly show my CDA badge. I reach out for Bena near the casino exit.

Bena bursts through the main entrance of the casino. She then uses Surge to ground the electrified rail. Next, she sprints across the grounded rail and jumps to the alleys. I pause to catch my breath. I am in awe at the alacrity and use of Surge by Bena. I brace myself for the same stunt. Part of the rail shocks me and I fly onto a roof. I dust myself off from the impact. I pick up Bena's Surge trace to continue the chase. I look down the alleys to see Bena reach a dead-end. I jump down to confront her. I turn on my evidence recording device and point a vibro-pistol at Bena.

I am out of breath but continue my protocol.
"Bena, I need you to stop, or I'll be forced to shoot. I need to take you in for questioning."
She refuses to listen to my reason.
"Question what? Do you know how vile the johns can be? Let me just be."
I continue my statement.
"You've killed someone Bena. Your crime scene seems similar to a murder we tracked awhile back. Are you affiliated with the Cloaks?"
She scoffs at the implication.

"The Cloaks?! Sister Solace was the last time there was any structure there. The new Cloaks don't want anything to do with Surge candidates. Furthermore, these johns deserve their fate. And I enjoy using my body for money for your information. It's my choice and my ownership. I'm not here to be some military lapdog like you either. Maybe I should join that new gang."

I ask with consternation.

"What new gang?"

She tells me about them.

"The Regiment. We Surge candidates should be free to do what we want. Keep thinking the CDA is for us."

I calmly explain.

"I know gang life. The CDA saved my life when my gang sold me out. You could come in and..."

Bena stands on guard.

"Then you know why I must do what I do. So shut it lady."

She shoots out a Surge blast at me. I instinctively fire my vibro-pistol. After firing, the Surge blast knocks me back. However, Bena is bleeding from her jaw where the vibro-pistol shot her. Before I can move, she is upon me with an auto-sword. It fully switches out at the press of a button. I calculate it is an old pre-Surge weapon. This explains the strange markings of the crime scene.

Bena breaks my concentration with a stab to my shoulder. I wince in pain and send a Surge blast to Bena. She absorbs most of the blast before it singes her multi-colored braids. She tries to pin me down, but I manage to wrestle out of it. I shoot another shot from my vibro-pistol. Bena gets up to strike again but then crumples to the floor. On the ground, a scan of her body reveals a hole in her chest. I fall to my knees. I stare at where the vibro-pistol shot went out. Then I stare at Bena in disbelief. I wish she let me help her. I file the Regiment information in my holopad for later research. I hope

that the CDA can produce something to find independent
Surge candidates. It is a difficult process. Thus, i wonder how
much the CDA forces Surge candidates to become agents. I
connect to Captain Yaa's frequency.

I gather my breath.
*"Captain. I'm going to send you the holovid recording of the
suspect. We found out who the murderer was for the john.
Seems consistent with the other homicides as well. The lady
had an auto-sword for non-cauterized killing. You'll see
everything in there. She was a talented Surge user."*
She thinks about my last comment.
"Really? What happened to her? Could she join?"
I hang my head low.
*"No captain. It was a shame she couldn't be kept alive. It was
me or her."*
She asks for clarity.
"You had to kill her?"
I answer truthfully.
*"Yes captain. She was a dangerous Surge candidate. Not up to
the structure of the CDA."*
She concludes our debrief.
*"I understand Afia. I'll review the holovid. Good job on your
first mission. Get some rest, you earned it."*

I ride the rail to the car park. While reflecting on my
night, I call Abeem.

She worries about the time and how I am doing.
*"Afia you've been out awhile. That was longer than expected.
Is the butcher still open?"*
I tell her.
"You're going to have to order it. This was a tough case."
She consoles me.
"Are you ok hunny? What happened?"

I reject her initial efforts.

"Babe, I'd rather talk about it in person."

She reassures me.

"I'll put the egusi soup pot on to boil. Then I'll get us some goat. Get home safe sweetie."

I smile in love.

"Can't wait to rest in your strong arms babe."

I realize Abeem will not be happy to hear about the battle with Bena. She can be overprotective. I also decide not to tell her about my flirtations with Laila. I analyze my case files. I see all the updates from doing well on my first case. Bena's mention of a reckless gang of new Cloaks makes me miss Sister Solace's leadership. I take a gander at Sister Solace's file. I think I'll check on her again. I put some afrobeats on my car speakers and drive to Abeem's complex.

End Chapter 15

****

Chapter 16: File 7 Maladies and Malfeasance

As an independent CDA officer, I receive a case about a missing military doctor. I gather information and research for the case. All leads so far point to kidnapping by one of the Tesano gangs. I decide that I must visit Sister Solace, the leader of the Cloaks. The Cloaks are the most adept gang at kidnapping. They primarily kidnap for indoctrination into their gang. As such, I think that Solace is a prime source of fresh perspectives. The only issue is that she is still in military holding for her previous crimes. Being at opposite ends of a gang war does not make for the best memories.

I read a note with a picture from Abeem about her promotion tomorrow. I admire her outfit and how elegant she looks in full regalia. Lately, I worry about all of her military events I keep missing. However, I know my extra work is worth it for my own impending promotions and merit. I tune my frequency for Captain Yaa to request for clearance into military holding.

I start off with some general idea of the case file.
"Captain Yaa. I've been looking into that military doctor's file. Kidnapping is often one of the Cloaks' vices."
She ponders about my idea.
"What are you thinking?
I offer a proposal.
"Well. Sister Solace might have a lead. She's in military holding but maybe I can see her"
She speaks incredulously.
"I'm doubtful. And don't forget Solace is still dangerous. But do you think this is the best way?'
I reason with her.
"It's all we have. I'm going to check into Rick's Cafe as well."

Captain Yaa concedes at my proposal.

"Very well, Afia. Because she's a military doctor, getting her back is of the utmost importance. I'll open up clearance for you."

I thank her profusely for the chance.

"Thanks captain. When I find something, I'll let you know."

I ride the rail to the Central military police headquarters. They connect to the military barracks and lab. It is the place where Abeem and the Accra military work. The military barracks are oppressive and plain, but the military police buildings are corporate and sterile. Most citizens fear the military police or MPs but ignore the military. Most of that MP fear is due to the ruthless Gifty Amoah. She dominates the city while still staying in the confines of the law. She'll do anything so most of us never rise above our station.

Both the central MPs and central military tend to help each other with Accra issues. Furthermore, the military deals with international issues and the constant influence of the Asante Empire. General Aku, the leaders of the Asante Empire, hopes to one day assimilate the Accra military into hers. Still, Accra holds onto its own army and military police force regardless of the general's influence.

Below, the military police headquarters lie the holding cells. Some of the most prolific of West Africa's criminals are held there. This is where Sister Solace resides. She is there for her frequent past crimes during her tenure as leader of the Cloaks gang. I pray to the Orishas that she is up for talking. The clerks of the holding cells scan me. I turn in my service vibro-pistol. I journey to Sister Solace's cell. I sit in front of her. She looks up and eyes me. Even in prison, Sister Solace manages to appear regal.

She smirks at my attendance.

"Ah if it isn't the prodigy, the new Voidess? O wait, you're CDA now. Interesting. But damn Afia. I haven't seen you in a minute."

She is already imposing. I meekly ask for her help.
"Well, I need your help on locating the kidnappers of a military doctor."

She reclines on her bench.
"Now why would you think I know anything about that? I've been in prison. Plus those new Cloaks aren't loyal. Not sure if they're up for my indoctrination style of kidnap and join."

I think about her explanation.
"Fair enough. I didn't think about that. But I figured you might have had some influence still."

She waves off the assumption.
"You would think. But no. When me and my true Cloaks got caught, the newbies ignored me. But here I am with no visitors but you"

I continue to analyze her words.
"Well if not you then who?"

She tells me to be more thorough.
"Go through the list dear."

I go through my thoughts out loud.
"Hmm, Ramirez and her Harvesters would sooner shoot a hostage than keep one. Techno Kids maybe for ransom, but they're too drugged out to not botch it. Hmmm Old Guard and Sirius?"

She smiles at my effort.
"You're doing well with this."

I bolt up with a puzzled look.
"Wait, do you actually know who did it?"

She laughs as if playing a game.
"I know something. I just know the Cloaks aren't involved."

I ignore her toying with me.
"Come on. This is serious business. It's a military doctor like I said."

She holds up a finger.

"Now Afia. Before I tell you anymore, you're going to make a deal for my release."

I shut her idea down right away.

"Hell no! I can get you some smokes but that's about it."

She tells me to consider my options.

"O stop. You know there's still no concrete evidence about the warehouse. You know damn well they can't pinpoint anything on me. Besides, what I tell you will be a good deed to clear myself."

I half agree with her.

"I'll think about it."

She turns back to her cell.

"Then good luck dear."

I give into her game.

"Alright, fine. You running the Cloaks would be better anyways. Those assassinations are filled with collateral damage these days."

She furrows her brow.

"Those cretins…Anyways, all the times I dealt with Sirius they didn't seem to hold hostages so much as transport them. So the doctor would've been found by now. Meanwhile, the Old Guard is well, old fashioned. Last time I checked, they don't always have the best corporate health insurance."

I surmise what to do for my next step.

"Hmmm maybe I could find a lead on them at Rick's."

She lays out everything for me.

"Say hi to him for me dear, but also tell him this code message 'Salt for Gold.' You'll get some help with that one."

I get up to leave.

"Alright, if this all goes well, you're back with the Cloaks. Hopefully, you can clean up their mess."

In the end, she is still nonchalant.

"We'll see. Maybe I'll do something new with them. Alright, chop, chop Voidess. Remember, "Salt for Gold.""

She gets up and turns away from me. She practices her weapon arts with nothing but her hands. She mocks me with a wry smile. I hope that she'll restore order for her Cloaks when she's out. I leave holding and travel to Rick's.

End Chapter 16

****

I speed over to Rick's to pilfer information. Based on Sister Solace's clues, I wonder if I can spy on the Old Guard gang. They're not my biggest fans. The old Jamaican bartender with grey locs and fuzzy beard, Rick, calls to me.

Rick greets me.
"Afia! Good to see ya' again! What ya' need?"
I whisper low to him.
"Salt for Gold"

He pauses, nods at both of his bartenders one after the other. He then goes to his back room. Nearby, I overhear two Old Guard gangsters. They are dressed in red steampunk clothing and rambling about their affairs.

The first Old Guard mutters.
"Just keep the contamination under wraps. You know how Sirius learns of everything."
The other Old Guard member agrees.
"Indeed. They can't know about the sickness. If they do, it will weaken us in Tesano. Hopefully we'll figure out how to help the other co-leader."
The first Old Guard takes a drink and thinks what's next.
"If not, we'll do what we always do."

Both Old Guard gangsters pound their gloved fists together and grunt. I realize that there must be an issue with one of the Old Guard co-leaders. The Old Guard travel in pairs. The same goes for their leadership. If anything happens to one of the co-leaders, the Old Guard tends to become disruptive. Before I can think more about the Old Guard issue, Rick returns holding a device.

He asks once more for reassurance.

"Ya' sure?"

I stay firm in my request.

"Yes, Salt for Gold."

Rick sighs and unlocks the device. He explains one of the features of the device.

"Be quick ye'? It be gone in a moment."

He hands me the device. It is a tablet showing the exact locations of the main five gang headquarters. Along with their locations, the tablet shows some data of gang activity. The reason why Rick can remain neutral becomes clear. He knows every aspect about the gangs' whereabouts and activity. I write a quick note of the five hideouts. I pay close attention to the location of the Old Guard hideout. I think about taking a picture. However, the table is most likely vaporware. Which means no photos can be taken of it. I Surge scan the image once more thoroughly. As I do, the imagery fades into the black nothingness of the device. Rick takes back the device and returns it to the backroom. I sense a commotion coming towards me. It looks to be a group of Harvesters, my old gang. Leading the group is none other than the old Harvester manager himself, Greene.

He is in a slightly drunk stupor.

"Well if it isn't traitor. Afia herself."

I warn him about my position.

"Careful Greene. I'm CDA now. And you know Ramirez will probably bust you up if you mess with a detective."

He drunkenly waves me off.

"Don't care. She's a loose cannon anyways. You sets us up back at the warehouse."

I ignore his remarks.

"Pretty sure you're on military parole Greene. Any slip up and you're back in holding."

He yells belligerently.

Greene lunges forward awkwardly. I hit him with a Surge blast that knocks him back into the bar. The other Harvesters release their arm blades. I trade blows and parries with the Harvesters while bar stools and glasses get smashed. Eventually, I lose control of the fight. The Harvesters are able to get the better of me. I place a protective Surge blast around myself. It disengages several cybernetic implants in the Harvesters' bodies. Greene's cyber legs lock and falter while he gets up. Amidst the chaos, a shotgun blast rings out.

Rick bellows at me and the Harvesters.
"Not again gyal! You keep causing me property damage! You lucky I like ya'! And Greene, ya' better stay right 'dere. My drones caught ya' nonsense. Those military guards over 'dere taking you back in. Sirius saw way too much for me to let you slide. Afia, ya' got what ya' came for, now get 'de hell out of 'ere."
I bow to him.
"Sister Solace says hi and thanks for everything."
He raises an eyebrow at me.
"Ah that's how ya' got it. Still, Afia, I no want to see you again for a while, ey?"
And with that, I take my leave.
"Fair enough. And Greene, you should've listened to me."
Greene roars as I pass.
"Damn you Afia!! I'll see you dead in the grave!"

I mark the Old Guard hideout on my GPS and drive there.

End Chapter 17

****

Chapter 18: File 7 Maladies and Malfeasance

While driving, Abeem calls into my frequency.

"Afia, check-in babe?"

I respond to her concern.

"Hey babe, I'm on my way to the Old Guard. I think I found out where the military doctor is. They might have kidnapped her for a reason."

She wants to help me.

"I'll round up a patrol to join you."

I tell her that is unnecessary.

"That's too much alarm for the Old Guard. Remember the gangs have a code and they could find out quickly about a military unit."

She threatens me with assistance.

"If you don't report back in 2 hours, I'm going there myself."

I laugh nervously a little.

"Jealous of my adventure? That's fair Abeem."

She reminds me of my absences.

"Good luck and you better be ready for my promotion tomorrow. You've already missed enough."

I can feel our recent tensions. I confirm again to be sure.

"I know I know. This work has been a lot."

She clarifies the importance of our bond.

" I know, but we still matter."

I trail off in my thoughts. I do not what to think about our issues.

"Yeah... I'll let you know how it goes."

I head towards a remote corner of Tesano with plenty of high rises. The area seems like an unassuming residential area. I follow a road ending in a wall with a tall building behind it. I send a pulse with my Surge to outline a garage with a special switch near a bench. I sit on the bench and the wall lifts. I enter the hideout and am met with a mini-grenade launcher by two Old Guard members. They lead me into their headquarters. I smell gunpowder everywhere. Several lights shine in my face. I get my bearings and see several Old Guard gangsters in high-class steampunk outfits everywhere. There are tight corsets, blouses, and jodhpurs galore. Behind the gangsters are rows and rows of explosives. This explains why no one wants to attack this base. One of the dual leaders of the Old Guard, Jojo, comes front and center. He dons an impeccable shape-up for his hair, a red vest and pleated black pants.

He speaks to me with caution.
"CDA Agent, what the hell brings you here? We heard someone has been snooping around looking for us."
I respond to his query.
"Pretty sure you have a missing military doctor."
He denies the accusation.
"Lies, you have no proof. We resent the accusation."
I interrogate him further.
"Well then why the hell were some of your people talking about contamination and where's your other leader…Jessi?"
He remains too stubborn to tell me anything.
"Hmmm those people will be dealt with accordingly." He then remembers CDA detectives use Surge. *"Say, you wouldn't know how to deal with the contamination?"*
I offer him an opportunity.
"Try me. You know as a CDA agent I do have the Surge."

Several voices in the headquarters mutter at the mention of Surge.

Jojo agrees to my offer.
"Hmmm. Alright Ms. CDA oppressor, I'll let you live if you can help Jessi with this contamination issue."
I correct him.
"It's Afia. Take me to her."

He leads me into a room with old medical equipment. On a bed is a woman, Jessi, Jojo's co-leader. Jessi appears frail. Assisting her is a military doctor.

I talk to Jojo.
"So, you do have a military doctor?"
Jojo urges me to focus.
"You can deal with us later. Right now we need to save Jessi. This is Dr. Adler. She's doing what she can."
I take a quick Surge assessment of the doctor.
"Doctor, are you hurt?"
She responds without issue.
"No, I am not hurt. But I've been trying to tell them that this military medical equipment isn't advanced enough to really work with Surge. I'm doing the best I can."
I investigate her research.
"That makes sense. The Old Guard isn't known for having many Surge people."
Jojo butts in to tell some history of the Old Guard.
"Some of us got hit with the Surge too. Due to our older age, it manifests like contamination of some sort. We did some digging. The records show that Dr. Adler is one of the best trained doctors in Surge experiments and research."
I lay out the consequences for him.
"I get why you did it. But it's going to bite the Old Guard in the ass with the military. Gifty won't like a medical civilian kidnapping."
He spits at the ground. A rare gesture for him.
"Fuck Gifty. This is more important than her rules."
I understand his stance. As such, I move to solve the problem.
"Jojo, do you think I can help with my Surge powers?"
He answers me.
"Well, that's why we didn't kill you outright. I don't know if you know how to help with this, but you're our best option."

I reminisce about Lacuna's death. It is tough, but it may help us.

"Years ago, I had a Surge mentor named Lacuna. I think she would draw power from others with Surge. It's worth a shot"

He makes the connection between Lacuna and me.

"Lacuna the Voidess? If you're her apprentice, then I'll try anything to keep Jessi alive."

The doctor tempers our expectations.

"Now Jojo and Afia; we have no idea the outcome on this. I don't want to be responsible if it winds up being negative."

Jojo maintains his confidence.

"Don't worry Doctor. Afia's got this!"

I locate the Surge in Jessi's body. I draw it slowly. The energy flows from Jessi to me. At first, it's very hard to even grasp the Surge. Then it rushes towards me. I cannot contain it. As the Surge comes out, a blast blows back everyone in the room. After some time passes, I shake off my dizziness. I scan the room. None of the equipment is working in the room. The Surge in my body seems to be back to normal. Jessi's Surge is not tracing anymore, but neither is her heartbeat. Jojo stands up to check on her. He notices her skin is better, but she is not responding.

Jojo begs Jessi to wake up.

"Jessi...Jessi...she looks healthier, but...ohh noo."

I report my grim findings.

"I'm not sensing Surge energy in her anymore. However, there's no neurons happening."

Jojo clenches his teeth. He points at me in anger.

"You did this, you vile abomination."

Dr. Adler tries to reason with him.

Jojo, we said we had no idea about how this would turn out. The Surge must have been the only thing keeping her alive."

He calls out to the rest of his gang.

"Old Guard! Don't let them escape! No one leaves here! You need to…"

A stern, but familiar voice cuts over him.
"Everyone stop where you are!"

Out of nowhere, Abeem walks into the light. Abeem drags a beat-up member of the Old Guard to where we are. While most focus on the bruised gangster, she trains her vibro-rifle on Jojo's skull. She is also carrying a detonator at her side.

She threatens the Old Guard.
"No sudden movements. Unless you all want this place blown up. If that happens the military police will be swarming here in seconds. The property damage won't be pretty. Lastly, I know you know what happens when a ranked official's military armor goes offline."
Jojo puts up his hands to stop his gang.
"Old Guard don't move. We don't want to upset the military now do we. Your move oppressor."
I finally question Abeem why Abeem is here.
"Abeem! How the hell did you get here?!?!"
She replies while still looking at Jojo.
"I told you I would come here myself if I didn't hear back from you."

A puzzled expression washes over my face. I am not sure how, but I'm thankful for her timing. The Old Guard surrounds us with guns. As they do, I grab the detonator from Abeem and grab Dr. Adler again. We slowly back away from the medical lab. Jojo keeps his gang calm while we exit.

He tells us off.

"Take the doctor and your military vermin out of here. I hope to never see either of you in my headquarters again. Old Guard, prepare the funeral rites for Jessi. We have a succession to deal with."

.   We get Dr. Adler comfortable in Abeem's car. Then I follow her back to our apartment.

****

Abeem's Apartment

I take a seat on a couch and smell the wonderful Ghanaian roast coffee. I admire some of her military fatigues and tapestries. Her place is always that of a warrior. There is low rhythm of some West African beats that I can not make out.

I relax comfortably and let my hair down. I think over the recent adventure.
 "Girl, that was a hell of a ride with that one."
She sets her coffee down and sits on the opposite of the couch.
"I hear you. The doctor is back in military care. She says she's able to help with any investigations you have in the future."
I thank her for the hookup.
"O I'm definitely kissing you for that setup."

I sit on Abeem's lap and nuzzle her neck.

As I get cozy, she gives me a stern talking to.
"Calm down. You would have missed my promotion if you stayed there. And you got into danger again."
I shrug at her mothering.
"Nature of the job."
She pushes me off of her.

106

"Afia, stop. I'll talk to the CDA. You need military help for your investigations."

I stand up and become stern myself.

"I don't need it. Besides, I took care of this case due to a good deal."

Once I say it, I immediately regret my admission of the deal.

She stares at me.

"What do you mean deal?"

I decide to face the music and tell her.

"So...Sister Solace is back in charge of the Cloaks. It's good though, you know. Maybe they'll finally have some order again."

She leaps up to meet me eye to eye.

"What the hell Afia?!?! You know the Cloaks are rough as hell. They used to kidnap military and citizens to indoctrinate them!"

I try to ease her anxiety.

"Only way this case worked hun. I have a direct link to her. The Cloaks have been haphazardly killing people. With her back in charge, this stability is better overall. She won't kidnap anymore. That was part of the deal too. Come on babe."

She takes her seat again, but remains grumpy. She sips some of her coffee.

"Fair enough Afia. But you can't keep surprising and worrying me."

With a straight face, I tell her the facts.

"You do the militaristic way. I do the CDA way."

She crosses her arms.

"I know and I still love you. Don't circumvent the military anymore, ok?"

I lean back into her arms until she opens them to embrace me.

"Ok then. I love you too. Now let's see what you plan on wearing for the promotion tomorrow?"

End Chapter 18

****

Chapter 19: File 23 High Profile Agent

On a high-speed train to Nairobi, I sit with Captain Yaa. We are meeting up with other CDA operatives from around the region at a summit. We are there to work intelligence and surveillance for several politicians. Post-Surge, it is amazing that politicians still exist. They're nothing but figureheads. Finance corporations and the military run most government installations these days. The summit hosts are some of the creators of the Constellation. It is an organization of the richest corporations. After the Surge, wealthy conglomerates set up the Constellation and its affiliates. I know one of those affiliates as Sirius. Their gang rehabilitation program gets financial assistance from the Constellation. Due to this, not everyone is at peace with the Constellation. While everyone is going to discuss global finance with the corporation, we will watch for something more sinister. In all honesty, we are all here to keep an eye out on any disturbances that would tank their expensive tech.

For me, this is exciting. It will be nice to enjoy a break from Abeem. Ever since, my run in with the Old Guard, Abeem is overprotective. Being nearly a private detective, I work more independently with my Surge powers now. As such, it's time away from her that she nags me about. But being one with the Surge is a feeling she can not possibly understand.

Captain Yaa brings me back to reality.
"Afia, you're daydreaming again. We're almost in Nairobi."
I apologize for my inattentiveness.
"Sorry Captain, I'm bored from the long ride. Thinking about Abeem."
She empathizes with me.
"I understand. I wish I was at home with my family as well. My husband makes the best yassa."

I recall her heritage.

"Right, you've got Senegalese and Ghanian cuisine right at home. Well Abeem makes the best egusi soup you've ever had. You should come by sometime. Or we'll come to you."

The idea is pleasing to her.

"That would be nice. Chin up Afia, we've got to keep a sharp eye out. You never know what Sirius or anyone else could be up to."

I acknowledge her orders.

"Yes Captain. You don't have to worry. The train is what is boring, not our mission."

I gaze out the window at the rows of Kenyan maize. This is going to be a fascinating time.

*****

Kenyatta International Convention Centre

The centre is one of the crossroads of the Eastern Hemisphere. All of Kenya's business acumen trade stocks and argue finance here. Today is special though. Thousands are here to hear Lily Cheung, leader of the Constellation, speak. As such, every food cart and hustler is at the entrance of the centre. The smell from the carts pleases my spirit. Meanwhile, the colors from the clothing hustlers blur in sync with the politicians' attire.

Captain Yaa and I check into our rooms in the centre. We send a few Surge pulses around to test the early safety of our room. We settle our bags and make our way to the auditorium. Lily's address to the politicians is in a few minutes. As we enter, I note all of the security surrounding the area. I even see some Sirius members scanning every bit of tech. To my knowledge, the high security makes sense.

Cheung's new ideas and policies for the improvement of the Constellation are controversial. She will be discussing Sirius's involvement in Africa and other aspects. There are many against this expansion among others. Many view the expanding grasp of the Constellation corporation as pure greed. Whether or not the corporation is beneficial is up to the individual. With these conflicting ideas, many terrorists and other interlopers are gunning for Cheung. She starts her speech right when Captain Yaa and I enter the auditorium.

Cheung clears her throat and steps up to the podium. *"Dearest distinguished guests, I welcome you to the Constellation summit!"*

There is thunderous applause. She waits until it dies down before she continues.

She grabs the sides of the podium and speaks her oratory magic.
"I'm so glad you are all here to hear of our great news. We here at the Constellation promise better infrastructure and control with the Surge. We hope to begin experiments that could use the Surge to improve our lives. These experiments will help us live stronger and longer. We will no longer have to rely on natural resources and AI."

Again, the crowd cheers at this statement. However, some of the audience is not too keen on giving up those avenues of commerce. Some are against the use of the Surge as well.

After the applause, she starts again.
"The Surge will become the tool that encompasses both. That is why today I come to ask you for your assistance in moving towards this model. With your help...

Mid-sentence, an explosion goes off in the Convention Centre. From what we can view from the auditorium, smoke blooms from one of the politician's rooms. Security scrambles to lockdown the politicians and check exits. Captain Yaa and I rush towards the explosion to investigate. There is barely any security there. Still, they let us through when we flash our badges. We discover that the whole room bears signs of implosion rather than explosion. These are the features of a gravity bomb. Captain Yaa allows me to lead the scan for traces of recent action with my Surge.

I tell her my findings.
"Looks like there was only one perpetrator here, Captain. This has all the makings of a gravity bomb. Most of the room got sucked into a gravity well."
She tests me on my skills.
"Indeed, it was one person, a cloaked figure, but they may have had help. Do you recognize that frequency?"
A revelation hits me when I read the frequency signal again.
"The universal Sirius signal! That explains how they got their hands on such dangerous weapons. We've got to tell Cheung and go check the files. There may be more terrorists."
Captain Yaa is uncertain of my hypothesis.
"I don't think Sirius supplied those weapons. Anyone on Sirius's neural link wouldn't attack Cheung. This is someone else. But you're right in that we should notify Cheung."

Before we can leave, Cheung arrives with a personal escort. Up close, I can see that Lily Cheung is absolutely regal in her patterned yet flowing dark yellow dress. Her skin is porcelain while her face is heavy with makeup. Meanwhile, her hair is shaved on one side but long, straight, and jet black on the other side. This is the most powerful woman in Hong Kong, and she models the appearance to back it up.

She greets us kindly.

"Ah, detectives. What have you found out?"

I report our initial discoveries.

"Terrorist actions. Possibly more and they're Sirius aligned."

She denies the accusation.

"Preposterous. Sirius would never do such a thing."

Captain Yaa sucks her teeth at me going with my initial hypothesis. She sets the record straight.

"You have enemies, Ms. Cheung. You're the North Star of the Constellation. Not everyone believes in the Surge. The weaponry may even be from Sirius. But we need more information."

Cheung paces the hallway.

"I just don't see how it could be unified Sirius members. You sure it's not some other faction? Maybe from…"

I shut down her attempt to blame other Tesano gangs.

"I know what you're thinking Ms. Cheung; but don't say it. Perhaps somebody learned how to break conformity."

Captain Yaa asks her more about breaking conformity.

"Has this ever happened?"

She reveals an interesting truth.

"Perhaps in the early years of the Constellation and Sirius? But it hasn't occurred in ages."

Captain Yaa thinks about her revelation.

"Well North Star, you have given us a great lead. My fellow detective and I have to do some research. We will let you know what we find. In the meantime, I recommend a lockdown for everyone here. It will help make sure people can be interrogated and protected."

She begrudgingly agrees to the recommendation.

"I don't like it but please be quick. We still have much information to get to the politicians."

End Chapter 19

Chapter 20: File 23 High Profile Agent

Communications and Data Room, Kenyatta International Conference Centre.

In the large data room, there are various CDA and others working to gather information. The place wanes in and out of activity from the coming and going of information. The captain and I find a data desk with a computer. We boot it up to begin our research.

Captain Yaa instructs me on the first steps.

"Afia, see if you can run a trace of any of the evidence. I'll try running the Surge through this supercomputer."

I comply with her orders.

"Will do Captain."

While we do our research a hooded figure enters the room and speaks with us.

The hooded figure startles us with conversation.

"Ah so I noticed someone tracing my Surge imprint."

In shock, I yell out to them.

"Who are you?! Freeze right there!"

The hooded figure puts their hands up.

"No need to be alarmed detectives. I'm nothing but a mere terrorist who wants to make sure Lily Cheung doesn't forget her country's origins. She promised that we would be using the Constellation's energy sources and not the Surge. This biofuel from Africa could restore the underclass of China."

Captain Yaa interrogates them.

"Exploitation of Africa? Neo-colonization again? Who the hell are you? Sirius? What are you planning?"

The hooded figure explains themselves.

"Well, you guessed right on Sirius. Though I'd say ex-Sirius now. Some of us have the power to resist conformity. My sister

and I resisted those years of torture. Can't tell you my name, but I will state my plans. As they all depend on Ms. Cheung's actions in using the Surge or not. Lastly, because I want to make this fun, good luck finding the other bombs."

I recall who the hooded figure is from the Techno Kid deal gone wrong years ago. - *"Wait a minute. I know you. Jiang?"*

Jiang expresses disappointment at the revealing of their identity.
"O...you. The young Surge girl who helped us then. Damn...of course it was you who Sirius wanted. But you shit since you found me out, it's time to go!"

I jump to restrain Jiang. I pass right through them. A hologram. I wonder how they are able to project their figure with no Surge trace. More Sirius technology? Again Captain Yaa snaps me back into reality.

She leaps to action.
"Afia, begin a Surge check on the whole convention center for those bombs. I'm going to see the North Star herself about the conformity. Also, you said you them?"
I sigh that there is too much to explain.
"Harvester times Captain. What can I say that would take a short time."
She sighs too.
"Then it's best for another time. Let's handle these bombs."

Abeem calls me on my frequency as we head out.

I can tell she is frantic.
"Afia?! Thank the Orishas you are ok. We heard about the implosion on the news. What is going on?!"
I am too busy to focus on her.
"I'm ok. We're connecting everything that is happening. There may be terrorists in the building."

She offers her military as usual.
"Do you need the military sent in?!"
I deny the notion.
"Calm down Abeem. Not everything problem needs the military. I know you're a little scared, but I need to get focused on work here."
She worries over me.
"It's more than a little scary. Please let me know you'll be alright."
I console her.
"Don't worry about it love."

Captain Yaa enters Lily Cheung's lavish North Star room setup. On the ceiling, a shifting constellation is on display with freestanding stars. There are several officers around her in defense.

The captain relays our new discovery.
"Ms. Cheung. We have confirmed that the terrorist, Jiang, is indeed a member of Sirius. There could be more potential gravity bombs throughout the convention center. We need to evacuate."
Cheung disagrees with her idea.
"Nonsense, we still have to give our information out to the politicians. And they really were a member of Sirius? Wait Jiang? Hmm, maybe Jiang Liu. They have a sister, Chyou. They could be part of that cell that left conformity years ago.
Captain Yaa asks for more information.
"Ms. Cheung if you have more info then by all means share it."
She finally relents the hold on her secret information.
"Years ago, when we were first experimenting with Constellation conformity, some Sirius members left and

wanted out. They tried to replicate the old Chinese Neo-Colonization model from the early 2000s. They want biofuel. They hate the practicality of Surge because it will hurt their pockets short term. I'm willing to bet those Liu siblings could be running things still. "

Captain Yaa thanks her for her honesty.
"This is helpful and might help us track Jiang. However, don't you think they could also be rebelling from the conformity itself?"

Cheung agrees with her.
"That could be a big reason. They always have wanted their own free will and mission. And that is to restore the China of the past rather than the Constellation of the future."

Captain Yaa folds her arms.
"Well then they would have extreme prejudice with the Constellation. Not just a different perspective, but rebellion. As such, we need to get you and everyone out of here immediately."

I interrupt their meeting.
"Captain Yaa! I'm picked up a coded frequency. It has enabled me to trace the Surge of the bombs and Jiang. They are moving towards the Ghana diplomat room! We need to move now. Here are the coordinates."

Captain Yaa demands Cheung to get to action.
"North Star, the bombs are going to go off now! Send the CDA and soldiers to these coordinates."

She sends the frequency to Cheung in order for her to send a large broadcast. The whole convention centre scrambles with the news of evacuation and bombs.

End Chapter 20

****

Chapter 21:File 23 High Profile Agent

Captain Yaa and I rush to the Ghana diplomat room. The door is locked. Through our Surge we sense someone in the room with tech. I kick down the door. We see Jiang finish planting their bomb. Captain Yaa blasts them with a wave of Surge. They fly into the wall opposite the bomb.

From the floor, they whisper their manifesto. *"Can't you see how much the Constellation wants to control everyone?! It's not just about me, but you as well . You have no idea what conformity is like. Death to the controllers! Long live the Liu family!"*

They hit a button for a gravity bomb to go off. Captain Yaa grabs the bomb and contains it with her Surge. I use my Surge sense to track for nearby bombs. Apparently, they're sequential. If we stop this one then the others stop from imploding. Currently though, the implosion of the gravity bomb is interfering with Captain Yaa's Surge. I try to help her contain it. Jiang limps out of the room in the chaos. They are met with Cheung and her security.
Meanwhile, the gravity well of the implosion warps reality. Captain Yaa's arm distorts with the gravity well. I use my Surge to limit the implosion to her arm. At once, the gravity bomb sucks her arm with the Surge in its gravity well and dissipates.

With my eyes wide, I yell to security. *"Someone get a medic in here now!!!!!!"*

I cauterize her arm from the bleeding with Surge sparks. She stabilizes herself while medics rush in. Cheung sends Jiang to lockup for questioning after their capture. During this, Captain Yaa blacks out from blood loss. A note on my frequency tells me that the other bombs are no more thanks to the efforts of the security and other CDA. The medic comes in and lifts the captain on a stretcher. I go with the medic team when they take her to safety.

In a medical hospital, Captain Yaa rests on a bed. A bandage covers her arm socket. I wait at her bedside.

I express my happiness that she is awake.
"Captain, I'm so happy that they can implement cyberware into your arm with ease."
She rejects the cyberware.
"I think I'm going to go with no cyberware. I don't want it interfering with my Surge."
I look at her funny.
"It will not Captain. You know it's ok for the repair."
She shakes her head.
"It's my preference. We'll see if I want it to be robotic one day. But for now, I'm just glad we were able to stop more bombs from going off."
I concede at her preference.
"Indeed, hell of a time working with you Captain."
And with that, she feels it is time for my promotion.
"As a matter of fact, I think you're fully capable of moving into the private eye sector fully now. You don't need to rely on the CDA or me anymore."
I leap for joy.
"Really?! I could finally give time to Abeem."
She smiles then continues her hard work as always.
"Absolutely Afia. Now where is Ms. Cheung? We need an update."

I call up Cheung on her frequency. She is already entering the hospital. She comes in with her bodyguards and media.

Captain Yaa berates her from bringing in the media.
"Get the media out of here Ms. Cheung."
She reluctantly agrees to do so.
"They make me look even better than I am, but that's fine. Without you two I would probably be dead. We have located a few other members of Sirius who have broken conformity. Apparently, you were right. They were Jiang Liu of the Lius. A family that broke conformity. Their sister's whereabouts are unknown."
I ponder about that loose thread.
"Hmmm they'll need to be tracked down."
Cheung alleviates my worry.
"Don't worry about that. The Constellation will seek them as needed. I have also sent a request for you both to get promotions and a stipend."
Captain Yaa thanks her for her support.
"Thank you, North Star. And thanks for dealing with the media."
I leave for an important phone call.
"Hey Captain and Ms. Cheung, I'm going to call Abeem to let her know what's up."

They both wave goodbye to me. I exit the hospital and ring Abeem on my frequency.

I tell Abeem the good news.
"Hey love. Everything is ok. We found the terrorists and I'm getting a promotion!"
She expresses her joy.
"Hey sweetie, I'm so glad you're ok! Who were the terrorists and ooo a promotion?!"
I update her on everything.
"Yes dear, I'm going to be a private eye, so I can set my own hours. I'll have more time to be with you. As for the terrorists, they were ex-Sirius members."

She replies to the updates.

"Hmmm I'll put that into the military files. And that's so exciting that you'll be basically an entrepreneur. Hopefully now you'll answer my calls and spend time with me more."

I roll my eyes but do agree with her.

"Yes, I'll try to be better. I hope to be in your arms soon my love."

End Chapter 21

****

Chapter 22: File 31 Afia and Abeem

I am my own private eye/detective now. I got a new government apartment in Tesano. I like being close to where it all started for me. I know Abeem wanted me to move in with her. Still, I like having this spot for work and hers for peace. She wouldn't understand. The weather tonight is not abnormal and I'm relaxing on my couch for a moment. I glance over at my cluttered office. I suck my teeth and ignore it. Next, I lean back and put on the Ghanaian Black Star football game. I sink into the couch.

An hour passes and a knock occurs at my door. Being independent, I get all kinds of randoms now. I miss the curated detective files. A lady with an afro-mohawk and tattoos enters. She's a tall Amazonian, lighter skinned woman. Her face bears some distinct features with hooded eyes, high cheekbones and a flatter face overall. She's panting and barely breathing.

She speaks through breaths.
"Is this...Detective Afia's... office?!
I respond calmly.
"It is. Please rest and have a seat. Who are you?"
She blurts out.
"The name is Khlori and I need your help. You've got to get the Techno Kids off of me and help me with a problem.
I repeat my instrucitons.
"Again, sit down Khlori. Why am I helping...what seems like a Techno Kid drug dealer?"
She speaks when she regains her energy.
"Not now. The Techno Kids think I killed one of their higher-ups with a bad dose. I received it from our usual supplier. I don't know what's going on. They're going to stomp out my crew, then go for me next. There is no way the gang will trust me!"
I rest her nerves.

"Slow down. Maybe this is an internal issue. So, let's see. The supply could be bad. And the higher-up got a bad hit from it. Has to be a big deal, right? Hmmm, the Techno Kids are going to break this on their sound system in Tesano soon. The Omnipotent One will probably be pissed. How much you going to pay me to deal with their wrath?"

She asks cautiously.

"Will you take drug money?"

I mull it over.

"...yes. I work for myself now so I'm not mad about it. Where are you going to get this money if you have no way to deal?"

She begs me to reconsider.

"If we can figure out, who did it, I'm sure the Omnipotent One will help you. I'll give you everything I have. I want out after this."

This is incredulous for me. I am not sure what I'm getting into. But I like it.

I curiously ask why chose me.

"An exit strategy too? Damn Khlori. This is going to be an interesting one. One more thing. Why me?"

She explains.

"You're not military and you're not gang affiliated. One would lock me up and the other would kill me. I had seen one of your ads at Rick's. So, I figured why not."

I laugh at the coincidence.

"Hah I'm surprised Rick still lets me post there. Guess he does enjoy my nonsense. Is the body still at your den?"

She hurries me along.

"Yes, but we've got to hurry. My crew doesn't know what to think and half of them are on Zela."

My eyes grew wide in surprise. The drug is very familiar to me. My girl Abeem's family associates with it.

Now I hurry her.

"Zela?! Damn let's go in my car. If any of them gets too high and anxious they'll expose you in a heartbeat with those antics. Why would you leave them!?"

She throws up her arms.

"I had no choice. I'm here for my crew, but I also need to worry about me."

We travel to Techno Kids' territory in Tesano; towards one of the many drug dens.

Khlori's Drug Den

Khlori and I arrive at the main drug den she works at. Abeem calls my frequency. I tell Khlori to go ahead without me.

Abeem brings up some information.

"Hey, did you know that one of the Omnipotent One's Techno Kids is wanting out?"

I'm surprised at the speed this reached gang news.

"The story broke already?!"

She continues.

"Yeah apparently some rumors were rumbling. Wait, what do you mean the story is out already?! Afia do you know something? You know to turn in drugs to the military. The Techno Kids hide it well, but if it slips out of their area we have to be on it."

I act nonchalant.

"Hey, remember, I work independently now Abeem. I'm just investigating in Techno Kids territory to see if I can find any leads on some dangerous Zela."

She lets out her anger.

"Zela is always dangerous. Serves them right for getting a hot shot."

I don't like her tone.
"Abeem!"

She reminds me of her family's past with Zela.
"Afia, you know how many of my family died on Zela. Don't forget. Anyways, I'll leave you to your investigation. Make sure to give me some accurate info so the military can apprehend them."

I half-heartedly accept.
"Sure, thing my love."

To think, being independent would give us more time together. Unfortunately, that's not the case. Apparently, people seem to enjoy a freelance Surge user a lot. I'm not going to lie about its liberties. I tend to crack an imported Tusker beer and sit in my office to get a break sometimes. Abeem is thinking about having kids. Meanwhile, I think our jobs are too dangerous for all that. Thus, I find myself being a loner. Maybe it's time for true independence...

Khlori snaps me back to reality.
"Afia, you coming in or what?! Come look at this."

I set foot in her drug den. The smell of the place reeks of unwashed clothing and sweat. There is a vat and cooling fridge for drug production. I see some cracked vials of the sapphire-blue Zela above the fridge. The use is recent. Most of her workers are explaining fantastical stories and not entirely there. Clear signs of transcending on Zela. Finally, I see a body that looks familiar. It is the large body of Nana. I track my Surge on him to see any other signs of foul play. It must only be the overdose.

I tell Khlori my hypothesis.
"Hmmm I once knew this man. Your assessment of an overdose makes sense."

Next, I recreate Nana's last steps with my Surge. He seems fine when comes into the den. The moment he checks the supply vat he keels over.

I explain.
"Looks like he went to check on your supply and sampled some. Must have been a hot shot. Wonder why no one else died."
Khlori thinks.
"Those vials are already packaged. They were already on Zela before he entered, and they were really nervous. They took some Zela to transcend a bit ya' know? The higher-ups are intimidating. Even if Nana is more lenient, he's still intense."
I'm well aware of Nana's imposing figure. Still, this means the issue was Khlori's supplier. *"Any ideas where your supplier might be?"*
She suggests.
"We can go back to the drug farm, and see?"
I like her thinking.
"I'll use my Surge tracing on some of the machines there to see if I can pick up anything. In the meantime, do you have an extra safe house?"
She replies.
"No."
I ponder a moment and remember.
"Then we'll have to use my extra custody house. Get your crew to Rick's. He'll know what to do if you show him my card and ask for lodging."
She turns to walk then quickly comes back.
"Ok. Before I forget, here's some of our stash money as payment. I know it's not in digital format, but here it is."

When she hands me the paper credits, I notice a bracelet on her wrist. It looks similar to the engineering ones my parents have.

I ask her about it.

"That bracelet. Looks like an old Kumasi bracelet."

With excitement, she replies and is happy to tell more about her history.

"I was born there. My parents gave it to me. They were engineers in Kumasi before we moved back to South Africa. We should have never left. Who knew that the Surge would renew the Apartheid uprising."

I agree and give grace.

"My prayers to the Orishas on that one. I know the Surge has had a distinct effect on South Africa.

Khlori continues.

"However, I have to ask. How did you recognize my bracelet?"

I state from my past.

I'm from Kumasi as well."

She bows to the Orishas.

"Kindred spirits. Anyways, I'll meet you at the drug farm later."

End Chapter 22

****

Chapter 23: File 31 Afia and Abeem

An hour later, I reach the drug farm. The farm is fairly quiet and security tech seems minimal. There are almost no cameras. They make up for them in the number of guards they have. I'm guessing they don't want camera footage of anything, so they go with regular guards. Then I see the true reason why they have no cameras. A full body scanner. It would flash Khlori or me in a moment's notice. Still, I can Surge scan it from afar. The data from the body scanner tech will give me access. The supplier's name is Abdul. From the scans, it seems like Abdul left a day ago. There are no files on Zela in the scanner, they are clear of information. To really see this farm, CDA gear helps, but my Surge will do. Wait, perhaps I can listen in from the body scanner. As I listen, I record everything on my holopad.

One of the guards speaks.
"Abdul has that cut out now doesn't he?"
The other guard replies.
"Yeap took out one of the others yesterday. This cut should take out the other two and the rest of their teams. He's going to get high up with Omnipotent One ay?"
The first guard disagrees.
"With them? Abdul is trying to take over. He's tired of them."
The second guard gets them back into focus.
"Ok. Back to checking the coast. Never know if one of Nana's crew will come in."

While I listen to their banter, I see Khlori walking up towards the entrance. Damn. She needs to stay outside and wait for me. I hope she doesn't blow our efforts.

Khlori saunters up to the first guard.
"Hey, I need to see Abdul."

The guard denies her.
"Abdul told us not to let you in."
She questions him.
"Why? You know I'll pass the body scan. Nana knows I'm good for it."
The other guard jumps in to answer.
"Hmmmm Nana? Didn't he just get reported as dead. He's your boss, but now he's dead. Are you trying to take over?"
Khlori ignores the teasing.
"Come on goons let me through."
Out of the darkness, Abdul walks up behind Khlori. *"That's not happening kid. So glad you're here by the way. Shame about Nana. You made this too easy for us. Now we don't even need to worry about how he died. Since you obviously killed him."*

Abdul grins mischievously. Then he pulls out a vibro-pistol. The guards join him aiming at Khlori. I step out of cover.

I yell at her.
"Khlori run!"

The moment she moves, I overload the body scanner. The explosion knocks both guards back. Khlori careens into Abdul. The force stuns Abdul. Khlori gets his vibro-pistol and aims it at him.

I place my hand on the pistol.
"You don't need to do that Khlori."
She stares at me.
"But he killed Nana. He was going to kill me."
I assuage her.
"No sweat, I got everything on recording. Don't kill him though. This evidence will help the Omnipotent One deal with him. Might even save our asses."

Alarms go off. The explosion stirs guards to move to our position. I grab Khlori's hand and run. Guards close in while we escape. Looks like the only way to get this evidence to the Omnipotent One is right now. Though I'm not sure how to get there.

I ask Khlori for help.
"Do you know how to get the Omnipotent One's place?"
She takes the lead.
"Absolutely!" She flashes a set of keys in front of me. *"C'mon we'll take Abdul's motorcycle to get there."*

We dash to a vacant lot that has a mixture of electric cars and bikes.. Khlori hops onto a bluish-grey motorbike. I jump start it with Surge. We speed off towards the Omnipotent One. Several guards pursue us on electric bikes. Khlori weaves through the drug dens to get to the main causeway. The guards smash through them to get to us. Several addicts fly out from the impact of the bikes. In one instance, a Zela fiend crashes into a guard and takes him out. We reach the causeway to the Omnipotent One. I fire my vibro-pistol at the guards, and I knock one of the motorbikes off course. I look back and see that one of our pursuers is Abdul. I tell Khlori and she increases her speed. There are still two guards and Abdul on us. One uses an elevated ramp to land on us.. Khlori hits the brakes. The guard lands in front of us. She then drives full speed into the motorbike. She kicks the bike on its side hard and the guard topples over with the bike. The Omnipotent One's palace looms nearby. We reach the front entrance of the palace and quickly get off. We sprint to the palace. I flash my CDA badge to be let in.

Abdul and his guard get off their bikes and vibro-rifles to shoot us when Khlori yells.

We stand frozen. The guards at the entrance also put their gun sights on us. Everyone is ready to shoot. I use a Surge blast to try and fry everyone's guns when a voice speaks out over a loudspeaker.

The voice acknowledges Khlori's earlier statement. *"Let them in!"*

All the guards and Abdul pause. The entrance guards escort us into the palace. Booming Techno Kid gqom music fills the space. Various addicts and Techno Kids dance around on Zela. Colorful lights and holograms bombard the senses. With my Surge, the sensation creates an almost double sensory effect. Thus, it is not easy to focus here. As such, this is one of many reasons why the CDA tends to leave the Techno Kids alone. We go deeper into the palace. In a more secluded hallway, orgies, sexual holograms and waiters carrying packets of Zela to various clients all move in a cacophony of delight. I notice all kinds of people here, businesspeople from corporations, politicians, military, Harvesters, Cloaks and more. Finally, we enter an empty room. The lights flicker on and spotlights shoot up to the ceiling. A platform descends with the Omnipotent One on it. Their guards give them a standing ovation as they come to the floor.

They bow to the applause.
"Thank you. Thank you! You're all too kind. Now what is this news you have about Abdul and Nana. And what is this oppressor doing in my presence. Though it is good to see you again dear."
I groan at the insult but tell them our story.

"No disrespect O Omnipotent One. I'm a neutral party nowadays. I'm here to set things straight and absolve Khlori. All I ask is for a promise of compensation to handle it."

They think for a moment.

"You drive an intriguing bargain, but I do owe you for help years ago. Very well. Let's see the evidence."

Khlori and I present the recording and holopad evidence. The Omnipotent One and the guards exchange glances. They proceed to take an assessment of everything.

The Omnipotent One paces the room and says,
"Call Abdul in here."

Abdul marches in with a smug look on his face.
"Yes, Omnipotent One?"

They waste no time in questioning.
"Where'd you get the poison? In my new Zela there is poison."

Abdul feigns ignorance.
"What are you talking about? There's nothing in there but pure...."

Before Abdul finishes his sentence, the Omnipotent One grabs their vibro-pistol and shoots him in the head. Everyone takes a step back. They then shoot Abdul's guard quickly after. Khlori and I are wide-eyed, uncertain of what comes next.

The Omnipotent One hands their gun to one of their guards.
"Handle this. And clean him up. I need a new supplier. I'll have Dijana cover Nana's territory." They make a call on their holopad. *"Hi, Dijana. Yes dear, you're taking over Nana's territory starting today. Don't use Abdul for your connect, I'll tell you why later. Maybe try those Senegalese traders that pass through Ablekuma?"* They hang up and go back to addressing us. *"Khlori, I take you want to be gone*

from this. Here are some credits to start you off. And here's your compensation miss Afia."

Khlori and I are still in shock from the Omnipotent One's moves. I nudge Khlori when I realize their forgiveness.

Khlori becomes aware.
"Wow, uhm o right. O thank you. Omnipotent One, how can I ever repay you?" She bows when she says this.
The Omnipotent One answers her.
"By leaving. You're a liability with the attention you've drawn and your lack of faith in dealing. You'll be shot on the spot if you come back here. And CDA lady…If you leak out anything about my operation, you'll also be killed. Military girlfriend be damned. "

I shoot them a stern glance.

They shrug it off.
"Don't look so surprised, I have ways of finding information as well."
Khlori exclaims about her second chance.
"With this I can finally be free and head to the Cape Coast to settle down. Maybe even revisit Kumasi!"
After mulling it over, I thank the Omnipotent One.
"I appreciate the funds. Take care Omnipotent One. And good luck with management."
They reply to me.
"We'll be fine once we eliminate Abdul's forces and his supply base. Ugh. This is going to cost me a bit, but this is better than the fallout. Now if there are no more issues." They pause before continuing. *"Then everyone take some Zela and let's keep the party going."*

The Omnipotent One gets back on the platform to plan all their changes. Their guards grab Abdul's and his crew's bodies to take them away. Khlori beckons me onto her motorbike as we drive back to my office.

I tell her the next steps.
"We've got to go back and make sure you have everything in order. Once we're done you can be on your way."
She is grateful.
"Thanks so much for doing this; really."
I smile at her gratitude.
"Anything for a kindred Kumasi spirit. Thank the Orishas for this meeting."

End Chapter 23
****

Chapter 24: File 31 Afia and Abeem

Upon arrival, my Surge senses that someone is in my office. The sense seems familiar. As I walk in I feel the presence of Abeem.

I call out in the dark office.
"Abeem?"

Abeem marches slowly towards Khlori and me with a vibro-rifle aiming at us.

She gives a demand unsmiling.
"Hand over the drug dealer Afia. She's in a military situation now. Zela peddlers need to be punished."
I can't believe her attitude.
"First of all, this is crazy timing. How did you know when we'd be here? We know who murdered Nana. It wasn't her, it was Abdul. The Omnipotent One has cleared her. I'm sending my files to the CDA. All is fine."
She doesn't budge.
"Hand her over. As for how I knew you'd be here, ever since the Old Guard situation I have had a tracker on you. You know I worry too much."
A rage builds inside me.
"You have a tracker on me?! How the hell didn't I notice it with my Surge? And why would you do such a thing?!"
She explains the tracker.
"It's old tech, there's a minimal trace that is only magnetic. It's hard to trace with Surge and linked just to my phone. But you must understand. I need to know you're safe. You're never home anymore. And hell, now you're allying with Zela pushers?!"
I try to calm my Surge from joining my anger.

"Abeem, you know I work for myself now. Therefore, I am not under the military's jurisdiction. But I still can't believe you tracked me. Where is the trust!? How are we going to have a family like this?!"

Tears well in Abeem's eyes. Still, she states her demand louder.

"You don't actually want one! Now hand her over. I'm done asking!"

An idea springs to my mind.

"Khlori, look out!"

I push Khlori out of my window, knowing she'll land on the trash heap outside. Abeem fires her vibro-rifle at her. I overcharge the rifle with my Surge, so it stops working. Abeem runs to the window, but I hold her back for a moment. She wrestles free. When she gets to the window, she sees that Khlori is long gone.

Abeem backs away and screams at me.

"Dammit Afia! You let a Zela peddler go away! I'm going to have to let the brass know."

I walk away from her.

"You do what you want. I couldn't let you mess up my deal like that. This ambush and the tracking... I tell you Abeem, it's not right." I sit on my couch and shake my head.

She attempts to justify her actions.

"Afia, you must understand that all of this is because of my love for you. I love you so I wanted to know your whereabouts. You pull away so I want to know what's going on. Plus, you know I also have to do everything by the military code."

I ignore her explanation.

"Well, I'm sick of it! I'm done. I've been doing better on my own anyways. You're getting in the way of my work and my Surge."

She pleads.

"Afia I-"

I stay firm in my decision.

"No Abeem. Enough, I need time to myself. You have your military and family stuff to work out."

She tries to hug me.

"But Afia, I still love you. Please don't shut me out."

I stand up and point to the door.

"Leave Abeem. If you ever want my respect again, you'll leave now."

Abeem walks out the door crestfallen. With tears in my eyes, I turn away from her. Still, in my heart, I know it is time for our separation. Still sad, I look out the window hoping that Khlori made it out. I also hope that another adventure in Accra is waiting for me.

End Chapter 24 and Part 2

****

Chapter 25: Pulse of the City (Part 3)

Accra, 2340, 15 years after the Surge

Most people forgot about the time before it. However, the historians and me like to keep up with the calendar. The calendar in the Christian world that is. Because we all know that religion is nothing more than an ancient belief system since it occurred. That "it" is the Surge and we're still not entirely sure what it truly is. But enough talk about the past. Let us talk about the now. I'm Afia Osuwu, a private detective with Surge powers living in downtown Accra. Being a detective in a city with no police force is a hell of an experience. At present, there is a serious crime I want to investigate outside of gang territory. At least, that's what the gorgeous woman at my doorstep tells me.

The woman finishes her explanation.
"And that's where I found him. My father was half naked and shot multiple times in Ablekuma."

That is a unique location for a crime. Ablekuma isn't gang territory. It's usually no human's land. The Surge hit that area hard. As such, it begs the question why this killing of an old man so far from gang territory. I know a Dr. Adler in the city morgue who could help me examine the body. I zone out in thought before realizing that the woman is still talking.

The pushy dame repeats herself.
"If you could please find out what happened, I could access his accounts. It would set you up with a nice sum of credits. Please just listen!"
Her yell snaps me back to reality.
"I heard you lady, don't be pushy."
The lady continues her analysis.

"I know what they say you can do. Why the other CDA detectives and you can figure out this information. And I also know you work alone."

I laugh at her appraisal of me.

"I guess everyone knows about my skills ey? They're better than the CDA I'd like to think. Alright I'll go to the morgue to check your old man's body. But, before I do that, 500 credits up front."

She looks down nervously at her holopad.

"I don't have that kind of money right now. But I swear when I go home; I can access my father's account."

I get up to return to my files.

"Lady that account has probably been hacked multiple times by now. They probably scanned his tech implant. However, I'll let you know, ms…"

The lady stomps her foot in frustration.

"I told you my name was Josephine."

I turn in surprise.

"You have a colonizer name, still? Such a shame for such a beautiful woman."

She defends her name.

"My father was a devout historian for the government. He loved old African-American heroes."

Her dad is a government historian? Maybe this woman is rich.

I accept the offer against my better judgment.

"Fair enough. With that name you should be doing this work like the lady you honor."

She acknowledges my acceptance and her namesake.

"Please."

I give her my tech frequency for contacting me.

"Alright, keep your frequency open, I can be reached at Z-368. If he's been hacked, you had better have some type of asset I can use for payment. I'm kind, but I don't work for free."

She gleefully butchers my name.

"Thank you, Detective Fiada!"

I correct her and wave her out.

"It's Afia, dear now on your way."

Josephine exits the door. I look out my window at the rainy sky filled with skyscrapers harkening back to our ancient Ghanaian empire. I think how crazy the Surge is for all of this. Catastrophic events, sometimes they create technological advances too. I also cannot forget the power of General Aku's reign. Her Asante Kingdom is the reason why we are a force in Africa again. .

Later that night, I put on my jacket and start my mission. The government obsession with rainfall needs to stop. They set the weather in our city sphere to rain for the crops all the time. However, it always shifts me into a depressing mood. I step out into the street, while neon cars and lights pass by. Brothels, drugstores, pharmacies, gun stores, and clothing line the sidewalks. Everything is a commodity in this hazy world of mist and grime. I make my way to the Kwame subway towards Legon.

End Chapter 25

Chapter 26

Dr. Adler's office.

Dr. Adler is an old friend of mine who helped me out of a jam a few years back. Her office is sterile and filled with bronze Benin sculptures. I know she is in the back with the fresh cadavers. There, I find Josephine's father fresh on the autopsy table. I realize that Josephine is the daughter of Lucius Baker. He is one of the finest military archivists around. That woman is loaded with money.

The doctor greets me when I come in.
"Ah Afia, good to see you. Do your thing. See if you can learn anything besides the vibro-shot wounds."

That is the signal to use my Surge. Every time I do it's a rush. Even more so, now that I can experiment, it feels even more powerful. My brain's neural synapses explode and mye eyes glow. Suddenly, the world becomes blue and white within a negative space. Details of Josephine's father's death are apparent through his body. An oval-shaped object is missing from his back pocket. There are internal injuries from beatings before the shooting. His muscles show signs of tension from walking out into the wastes of Ablekuma. There is also a trace of the Surge around his beatings. This faint amount is very odd, but I keep that to myself.

I explain my discoveries.
"This old man had 'something' that people wanted from him. As there appears to be a missing object from his pants. He was beaten before he was shot. However, all the vibro-shots are from the same gun. This was a personal hit, maybe not a gang hit.

The doctor provides more context.
"Hmmm, but there were groups of footprints near the site.

I disagree with her idea.

"Even still, it's not usually how a gang would operate. Civilians are usually only in a crossfire. Not execution style.

The doctor persists in her theory.

"But might the gangs want that something? Could be important. Maybe it was just a few members of a gang."

I agree with part of her theory.

"Possibly, but most gangs don't work like that unless they have internal conflict. I'll check the archives in Central first. Maybe I can figure out what could be so important."

She is taken aback by my idea.

"How the hell are you getting into Central with the military posts? Your detective background doesn't give clearance anymore. You're not CDA."

I give her some confidence.

"How could I forget? They hound me weekly to rejoin. But don't worry I have an inside."

She asks a request.

"Care to share the connect? I would love some military-grade medical supplies."

I shut it down.

"Hey, I pay you to let me see the body before the military. And I don't have that level of connection."

She is not buying it.

"You sure?"

I relent to her persistence.

"Look if I find anything I'll let you know."

She takes that as a yes.

"Some amphetamines would be lovely. It's rare these days. However, the military often can procure relics of the past better than anyone."

I stare at her in wonder.

"A rare pre-Surge drug!? No promises."

I pick up my car from my apartment. Then, I speed off to the outskirts of Central. I am searching for my old lover, Abeem. She is military and someone who surely owes me a few favors.

****

Abeem's Condominium

Abeem lives in a small, gated community. It's a change from our old luxury apartment, but it's closer to her family. I walk up to her condo. Anxiety courses through me. We're not the best at communicating these days. I breathe deep and knock.

When I knock, I call her.
"Abeem!! So good to see you again. How's the family? I've got the deal of a lifetime for you, if it pans out."
A tall muscular lady with cornrows opens the door and sees me. She immediately tries to close it.
"No Afia, not again, no way! You wanted nothing to do with me."
I beg for her help.
"Aw come on now, this mission is not just my reward. Apparently, I just got done Surge scanning a dead Lucius Baker."
She realizes how important Lucius is.
"The Lucius Baker? How did you come across that crime?"
I continue to beg for help.
"His daughter. She could make us rich. But I need to get into the archives at Central."
She thinks my efforts are in vain.
"The archives? Most of that information is on the internet. No one uses the archives. Unless you want to research some relics."
I smile at her statement.

"And those relics are precisely what I need."

She is considering my idea carefully.

"How much money we talking?"

I appeal to her question.

"We'll have to see what we gather from archives. Still, it's better than your military pay. Hell, you can support your family even better."

She counters with an impossible request.

"That's all well and good, but how about you come back to me?"

I immediately deny her request.

"I don't know about that deal. It doesn't seem to be one I can fulfill."

She is saddened but agrees to help.

"Disappointing. Dammit Afia...this is the last time I do this.

I thank her exuberantly.

"Yes! Abeem, you're an Orisha! I can get us in with my Surge, but do you know the layout?"

She lays out a plan.

"Yes, we can use your Surge or my access. Let's do it tonight. We'll head in through an underground entrance the military waste lines head out from. Then I can show you how to get through the archives secret access."

I am ecstatic. I ask about Dr. Adler's medical supplies.

"Oh, secret access? Maybe we can find some extra information there. Side note, do you have any extra medical supplies or drugs?"

She gives me an angry look.

"Don't push your luck, Afia."

End Chapter 26

****

Chapter 27

Military Central Archives in Downtown Accra

At midnight, we survey the Central archives military compound. My Surge senses sharpen to analyze the area. Abeem leads me through the military escape route. The route connects to all the buildings in Downtown Accra. However, only military personnel can navigate them properly. We proceed to the back entrance of the Central archives. While there, we see that a couple of guards are positioned.

Abeem tells me her knowledge of the guards. *"The guard shift changes every hour at the entrance. Once inside, we'll be able to dodge soldiers according to the electronic map. Any ideas on security cameras?"*
I laugh at the question.
"Why would you ask that? You of all people know my powers can handle that."
Abeem scoffs at my teasing.
"I don't know why I even asked. Forgot who I was talking to." I spark a little Surge at her. She gets close. *"Stop playing around. Look for the guard change."* We wait for a moment, then the guard shift occurs. *"Alright there's the change, let's go!"*

We enter the back entrance quickly. I reach out to Surge burst the next entrance lock. Abeem puts my hand down and produces a spare military key card. I nod my head and we make it through. We tie bandana masks to our faces. This makes us appear as criminals instead of government officials in case anyone sees us in person. While we walk to the elevator, I use my Surge senses to see the circuitry of the building. I locate the camera circuits and adjust their live feed. This uses a great deal of my power to stall the cameras. I become a little faint from the exertion. I brace myself once we get to the elevator.

Abeem checks on my condition.
"Are you okay?"
I stand up straight with balance.
"I'll be alright once I reach equilibrium. Come on, we don't have much time to reach the archives before the cameras reset."
She agrees with my urgency.
"Well then let's hurry."

We continue to dodge guards and cameras. Still, I remain suspicious of everything. After passing what seems like miles of stark and bleak corridors, we are at the archives.

Translucent gold lines the floors and walls. Through the lines you can view the main part of the archives from every angle. Holobooks fill the archives' stacks far as the eye can see. I run immediately for the search directory to single out information on the oval-shaped image I remember. The database doesn't recognize the image. Abeem uses her military access code to reveal the classified files. The floor lights up with a blue line guiding me to the holobook we're looking for.

Abeem makes a remark on the section we're going to.
"The holobook is under the secret files on Alien Research? Are there alien possibilities with the Surge?"
I shrug at her question with confusion. I pull open the holobook's files.
"Hey, I'm just following my research."
She persists.
"Yes, but I thought this had nothing to do with aliens."
I read some intriguing information.

"You never know. The holobook says that the Surge was most likely caused by an anomaly from space meeting an ancient race."

She reads over my shoulder and refutes the book.
"This is really a bunch of post-Surge nonsense."

I then find the most important piece of information in the holobook.
"Hold on now. The Surge occurred in multiple places at once. All of these places have specific ancient historical civilizations – Olmecs, Asante Kingdom, Sumerians, Bantu, Shang Dynasty."

She is incredulous.
"What?!"

I flaunt my historical knowledge.
"You know I'm a historian. Anyways there are central points there that denote similarities to ancient civilizations coming in resonance with that comet that was passing through."

She throws up her hands in disbelief.
"So, everything just happened?!"

I give a deeper explanation.
"Well no. It states that the new inventions and materials being made before the Surge, made this harmony easier. Which is probably why the Surge occurred in the Atlantic Ocean. So basically, the missing oval piece is known as the Conduit of Power."

Abeem scrutinizes the checkout history of the holobook.
"Hey look at that. This holobook was used recently. Must have been someone with military access. There's a military entry several times with one person and then one that looks like it was hacked about a week ago."

I remark at the consistent reader of the book.
"That's interesting. It says the multiple entries…were by the military historian Lucius Baker. That's Josephine's father!"

She continues my ideas.

"Hmm he must've looked up this research then. He's not the only researcher, the one from a week ago says The Regiment."

I recognize the name.

"Hmmm the Regiment. I hear rumbles about that being a newer gang. Most people in the gang have transitioned. Might even been a Surge user or two, so I've heard."

She joins my excitement in this discovery.

"This gang must have wanted the power that Lucius held. The Conduit probably amplifies the Surge."

I note everything in my holopad.

"Well time to put this book back."

When I put the book back, the blue line on the ground turns red. Alarms blare everywhere. The holobook locks in my hand, showing an alarm trigger.

Abeem turns around to look at me. Her expression is one of shock.

"The Regiment must have hacked this book when they checked it out! We tripped a damn alarm trigger lock."

I scan for an exit. Then I pull her with me.

"Abeem, let's go quickly before the guard shift changes."

We race through the corridors. The security cameras slowly return to power. I try to use my Surge to depower the closest to us. We dash and dodge guards to reach the back entrance as fast as we can. However, when we get to the back hallway we see the new guard shift conversing with the current group. We can't wait. Abeem runs full throttle to the exit. She barrels into the first guards, knocking them over. Quickly, I follow her to the escape route. We don't stop moving until we are back at my spot.

Both Abeem and I catch our breaths. I log in the information I got from our experience into my holopad. Abeem paces around my apartment.

She is upset and tells me her frustrations.
"Dammit Afia! Now the military will discharge me in a heartbeat."
I remind her of our disguises.
"They may not know it's you. We had bandanas that would mask digital scanning."
She holds her hands on her cornrows.
"Argh, my ID is still connected to the coding in the building."
I suggest hacking.
"No worries, we can hack it out."
She is not a fan of it.
"Damn you Afia! That's going to require some work."
I tell her it will be fine.
"No worries. I can probably use a CDA connection to deal with it."

It's moments like these, that I miss having my old hacker friend Xochitl with me. Still, the CDA can do a quick wipe.

Abeem calms down a little.
"Anyways, what the hell do we know?!"
I am ready to move on and lay out the plan.
"Well first of all, maybe we can head to Tesano. Maybe grab some information from Rick's?"
She cringes at the sound of Rick's Cafe. However, she's on board to see this through with me.
"Alright Afia, you're on for Rick's. Ugh. Let me change. I can't wear military clothing there."
I lean back on the couch.
"Cool, something in my closet should work with you. Don't worry I won't peak."

She stares at me with a lack of humor. I laugh and she goes to change. I think of ways to find out more about the Regiment gang.

End Chapter 27
****

Chapter 28

We drive straight for Rick's on the main thoroughfare. The neutrality of Rick's never gets old. Rick may chide me for the fights I get in, but he is always happy to see me. Still, I'm glad Abeem is not wearing military gear. Once inside, the usual smell of palm wine and smoke fills our nostrils. We walk to the bar and check in with Rick to see what gangs are present.

I ask Rick a question.
"Hey Rick, who's in?"
He greets Abeem and me.
"Afia! Good to see ya'! And yere friend too. Well the Cloaks be in, but so is 'dere leader, Sister Solace. So ya' know they won't tell ya' not'ing. Techno Kids and The Old Guard don't know shit. And o, hey be careful of the Harvesters gyal. Ramirez is here with ya' old gang."
Abeem frowns at the mention of Solace.
"Hmmm we should stay clear of Solace. I don't want to deal with-"
Before she can finish, I blurt out my reaction to the mention of my ex, Ramirez.
"Ramirez is here?!"
Rick nods about everything.
"Yes so be careful. Try not to start any trouble with ha' or yere old rivals 'ey?"
I barely hear his warning. Instead, I try to learn about the Regiment.
"I'll try. Hear anything about the Regiment?"
He states what he knows.
"Check with Sirius. Only t'ing I know about 'dem is 'dey keep to them. 'Dey rarely show up here. I have no clue where 'dey are."

Abeem and I take a seat to formulate a plan to make a deal with Sirius.

Abeem starts questioning me.
"Wait, how don't I know about you and Ramirez? And you were in the Harvesters? Who rivaled the Cloaks? "
I wave her off. I avoid the topic of my life before being in the CDA.
"Another time, another life, before the CDA. Ramirez is an ex of mine."
She persists.
"You used to run in a gang? I thought you were just a civilian."
I change the subject.
"We'd do best to ignore it. Now let's go chat with Sirius. A promising reward might work in their favor."
She grabs my hand and sits me down. She is not budging from this topic.
"Hold on now. Tell me about your past, Afia."
I give her a quick rundown.
"I used to use my Surge powers for profit with the Harvesters. You may have heard of the Voidess or this Harvester girl with Surge powers. Yeah, my mentor was Lacuna the Voidess and I was the girl with Surge powers. Unlike most Harvesters, I had no cyberware. So, you wouldn't even have known I was a Harvester when you met me. Originally, I had wanted to take on my mentor's mantle. I wanted to help the Harvesters come to power; help them as the Voidess. But then Ramirez and I fell out after we lost her brother and Lacuna to the Lome military."
She puts a hand up.
"And after that is when I met you. Hell of a story Afia. Someday you better tell me more."
I stand up and nod.

"Come now, let's go get what we came here for."

We walk to a few Sirius gang members. One of them switches on their cybernetic eyes. Several streams of data and calculations trace across their eyes.

After processing everything, they speak.
"You have come looking for The Regiment?"

I pry for more knowledge.
"Yes, do you know anything about them? I'm looking for something."

They wonder about what I'm looking for.
"What is that something?"

I refuse their request.
"I can't tell you that."

They start to walk away from me, turning off their cyber eyes.
"This is finished."

Abeem interjects.
"Wait, does the name Lucius Baker ring a bell?"

I glance at her with disapproval. She gives me a look pleading for me to follow suit. I her strategy is right.

The Sirius member's cyber eyes light up again.
"The Lucius Baker. The once famous old-world scientist turned Surge researcher. Based on our data, he lived well below his means. Furthermore, it's showing that he has a vault worth...a lot."

Abeem smiles.
"Well, we're working with his daughter. She hired us."

I realize that Josephine Baker is one powerful connection.
"Then we can do business?"

The Sirius member agrees and shares their information.

"The group you seek often wears all white with purple hooded robes. There were traces of them on the fringes of Tesano. Seems our cameras last picked them up going underground, literally."

I start negotiations.
"What percent works for you?"

They say their first offer.
"40."

I find it too much.
"That's insane!"

Abeem gives a counteroffer with some extra sweetness.
"30 with some military-grade medical supplies."

I stare at her in disbelief.
"So, you did have some. I thought I could use that for my doctor."

She ignores my teasing.
"This feels more important."

The Sirius member watches our dialogue and interrupts us.
"If you two are finished, It's a deal. As always, if we don't receive our payment and supplies, you will both suffer the consequences."

Once we finalize everything, Ramirez joins our negotiation with her Harvesters gang.

She circles Abeem and I. She teases us at first.
"Afia, it's been ages, hasn't it?"

I keep my composure for now.
"It has been. I'd like to keep it that way. Go away Ramirez. I want nothing to do with you."

She mocks my attempts.
"Mentirosa. You sure? This your new novia? Watch out lady, she might turn on you."

Abeem squares her body in front of Ramirez.

"You watch your tone, Harvester."

Ramirez backs up a bit. She is a little cautious around Abeem.

"I got no quarrel with you. Anyways, it's good to see you Afia. Care to share the information you just got."

I shut her suggestion down immediately.

"No way Ramirez."

She basically tells me to me fuck off.

"Bien. We'll talk to Sirius ourselves. Then we'll take what you find."

Ramirez walks to the Sirius lead. All the gangs in the bar tense their muscles for a fight. They are listening to our exchanges and know our bad blood. Abeem grabs Ramirez's hand to stop her. Abeem beckons me to help her. When I get closer, Ramirez's blades protrude from her body. In a flash, Rick's bar erupts with blades and fists flying. While Abeem duels with Ramirez, I fend off the other Harvesters. The Cloaks and Sister Solace jump at the opportunity for a rumble. Her Cloaks spread out to challenge everyone. The Techno Kids blast their music. Lastly, The Old Guard leaves the bar. Pretty soon, I bring out my Surge to deal with the Harvesters' and their cyberware. The action continues haphazardly. Tables tip over and some bottles break. I grab Abeem then use a table as our cover. Suddenly, a shot rings out and everyone freezes. Rick locks all guns from firing the moment you enter, so we know it's him.

He berates all of his patrons.

"Look at all ya'. Ya' know my bar is neutral ground and not here to be conquered. If ya' have problem, come deal with my turrets."

Rick's turrets point towards everyone. It is a miracle he did not shoot all of us yet.

He then turns to address me, Abeem and Ramirez.
"Now Afia. Gyal, I'm going to have to ask ya' both to leave for now. Every time ya' come in here, shit hits the fan. I don't get it. And Ramirez, take yere Harvesters elsewhere too. Machado would be ashamed. The rest of ya' chill out and get some food."
Sister Solace toasts to him.
"Here, here Rick. Order up Cloaks. Take care now, Ramirez and Afia. Good to see you're still the troublemakers that I remember."

Both Ramirez and I flip off Sister Solace while we leave. The rest of the gangs and CDA agents go back in good spirits to drink and eat in peace. Ramirez and her Harvesters leave us alone for now. Abeem and I stroll back to my car. I open the door to my car and pick up a signal on my frequency. It's the Sirius lead.

They confirm with me.
"Just to confirm. Our deal is golden. If you betray it, we know where you stay Afia Osusu. You as well Abeem Yeboah. Contact us when ready."

We make tracks for the underground lair of The Regiment.

End of Chapter 28
****

Chapter 29

On the fringes of Tesano, there is nothing but abandoned buildings. There are no businesses here. Due to that, most of the gangs never come here. There are not enough civilians to make a good profit here. As such, Abeem and I ponder if Sirius is telling the truth.

We go to the location from the camera. The entrance to the lair of the Regiment appears to be hidden from us. Sirius might know the location, but Abeem and I wait to figure out how to enter it. While waiting, we see a few hooded figures come out of the shadows. We hide and observe them from a burned-out storefront. Soon, a burst of electricity comes from the hooded group. The lair opens. This gives Abeem and I a moment of pause. The Regiment are Surge users. The CDA will want to hear about this.

Abeem wants to learn more too.
"Afia, wait. I always knew there were more of you, but I thought they were all registered detectives."
I shrug.
"I guess these ones didn't want to register. More importantly, this means I can get us in."

The Surge crackles from me when I charge the front door. The lair opens to us. The atmosphere feels comforting. There are purple banners with white streaks everywhere. The lit floor and walls show Surge flowing throughout. We follow the Surge lines towards what we hope is the main hall. We finally enter a larger room. My Surge can sense the oval object nearby. We see the Conduit. Strangely, it floats in the air and moves closer toward us. As it does, the lights in the lair go on. Surge-powered lighting and holovids shine in our faces. Abeem and I take notice of our surroundings. We see purple hooded figures everywhere. The figure with the Conduit steps forward. Abeem and I prepare ourselves.

She introduces herself. She removes her hood to reveal glowing blue eyes. It seems that the Surge affects her body. Besides her eyes, her afro has streaks of the Surge in it as well. Some other members of the Regiment show similar features, but not all. Due to her transformation, I surmise that she is the leader of the gang.

Before we can interrogate her, she does the same to us.
"Come now, if we have the Surge infused in our lair, you know we could see you the moment you entered. Why on the Orishas, have you come here?"
Abeem aims her vibro-pistol at the leader.
"To arrest you! You and your Regiment are under arrest for the murder of Lucius Baker. Furthermore, you have also committed the crime of accessing military secret files. We know that's where you got the Conduit!"
The Regiment leader ignores Abeem.
"We of the Regiment couldn't care less about your regulations. Now that we possess the power of this Conduit, we will use it to augment our power. When the time comes, not even General Aku and her oppressive military will be able to stop us."
I join Abeem and unholster my vibro-pistol.
"That's a fine idea for your Regiment. Still, we're going to need that Conduit and all I need is one shot for that."
The Regiment leader stays firm in her response.
"I have no idea how you expect to fight us with those. Norieta here would have you both flat in seconds."

She motions towards a tall, voluptuous member of the Regiment with a two-strand twist style in her hair. The tip of her spear swirls with Surge energy. Abeem and I look at her then the rest of the Regiment and see several more Surge spirals aimed at us. We relax a little but keep our pistols towards the leader.

She continues her warnings.
"Now that you know what you're up against, I know you will listen to reason. To be fair, we are all part of the Surge. It's also a surprise that you, dear CDA detective, don't wish to join us. You know how much we are considered outcasts in society. Shockheads if you will. As General Aku loves to call us, before she tortures us. She makes sure that we stay oppressed because of our connection to the Surge. O how I hate that bitch. Lastly, I know being a detective pays the bills. But here you can truly live how you used to; free from the military's reigns."

Honestly, I agree with her commentary. I pause for a moment.

Abeem glances at me.
"You would want to come back to that?"
The moment passes and I know where I stand.
"She speaks a lot of truths. But my past is gone. Thus, we've got to get that Conduit and then get back to Josephine."
She nods, but then questions my suggestion.
"Shouldn't we return it and these people over to the military?"
I disagree.
"No, they are not experiments. Nor are they criminals for Gifty's military police gang. My job is to solve problems and cases."
She faces me and prepares to argue.
"Well Afia—"
The Regiment leader stops our bickering.
"I grow tired of your banter. Prepare to be eradicated and wiped from existence."

In that instance, bombs go off throughout the lair. Fighting breaks out between the Regiment and unknown assailants on the edges of the main hall. I see several flashes of metal and dark outfits…Harvester…Ramirez! How are they here?!

Ramirez yells out.
"Harvesters, enjoy the fighting! But leave the leader and the two neutrals to me!"

Meanwhile, debris falls from the collateral damage of the explosions. Several pieces separate Abeem from me. One of the pieces hits the Regiment leader. The impact forces her to drop the Conduit. In the confusion, I dive for the Conduit. When I recover it, I glance around for Abeem. However, I can't find her in the chaos. I scramble for the exit. Before I can reach it, I can hear the clinking sound of Harvester blades.

In the exit corridor, Ramirez calls out to me.
"Afia, what did you find mi amor?"
I turn around and find that we are alone.
"Ramirez I'm not telling you a damn thing about what I found so just back off!"
She spins a story to me.
"How come? We used to be so good together. Why did you have to go and mess it up with Machado and Lacuna?"
I know this lie and shut it down as always.
"You know damn well that wasn't me. You set me and Xochitl up."
She scoffs at me.
"Diablo. I saw no other option. So, we do what we must. Outside of that, how about an offer? It's been a while since the Voidess has helped the Harvesters."
I cross my arms.

"That's not what you're here for. You and I have been through enough. And I want no part in your harvesting schemes. You'll do anything to get what I found."

Her cyberware comes to life.

"Shame. I see I'm just going to have to take your find by force."

When I charge a Surge blast, the Conduit recognizes it. The power it sends to me amplifies my blast. A huge pulse knocks back Ramirez, opens the exit and cuts the light in the corridor. I'm too high on adrenaline and modified Surge to take stock of what of the blast. I barrel out of the lair and into my car. I contact Abeem's frequency and receive no response. I speed off towards my apartment.

Next, I call Josephine on her frequency.

"Josephine, this is Afia. Meet me immediately at my apartment. I think I found out everything that happened."

Her voice sounds more at peace.

"That's great news! Who was it? Did he have anything with him?"

I urge her to meet me.

"No time for that now. Just meet me asap."

I leave the grime of Tesano. The various mixing of afrobeats and electronic music from the Techno Kids' speakers wanes as I leave.

End Chapter 29

****

<u>Chapter 30</u>

My apartment door slams open. Josephine enters. She appears flustered yet hopeful.

She asks immediately.
"What have you found?!"
I sit up straight in my chair to tell her the news.
"Your father was killed over an object called The Conduit. I think it is something related to increasing Surge power."
She takes a moment. Then she asks me about his killers.
"Who killed him?"
I continue with my message.
"It appears to be the smaller but deadly Surge gang, the Regiment."

She paces around my apartment. She attempts to speak then stops.

She sits down and stares at me sternly.
"Where are they and how will they…"
I pause her thinking.
"Stop right there. We're not doing any harm or full arrests yet. I think you need to look at this Conduit first. Maybe it will ring a bell."

I bring out the Conduit. It reacts heavily to Josephine. Josephine's whole body glows to glows blue. Blue angelic wings sprout from her body. She screams out from the metamorphosis. All I can do is stare in shock. Then I realize what is going on. I try to calm her. Before I can, a hologram of

Josephine's father materializes. I recognize Lucius Baker's research outfit.

The hologram eyes Josephine then speaks.
"Hey Josephine. Please don't be alarmed. If you found this, honey, well that means I'm dead. Anyways, I must tell you that you are a very unique person. Josephine - you are one of the original Seraphs of the Surge. While select people have received the gift of the Surge due to hormonal changes or pure luck. Some people became Seraphs, people who are linked to the essence of the Surge itself. Apparently, the Surge occurred when the "ghosts" in the machines or AI around the world achieved singularity. However, all that power couldn't be contained; thus, creating the Surge. I believe that this Surge was the natural result of the evolution of technology. Not all "ghosts" in the machine disappeared though. A few transferred to people and became Seraphs with unbridled power. However, I learned that this power was locked without the Conduit. The creators of the Conduit were trying to bring about the singularity. I had hoped to learn more in order to help you control your Seraph powers before I died. But with my fate as it is, I hope that if you find this you will learn to control them. I no longer must dampen your powers anymore. You're free to fly like you were meant to."

The hologram hums for a moment then disappears. Josephine and I are in awe. We take account of her father's explanation of everything from the Surge to Seraphs and The Conduit. Josephine weeps from her father's kind words. She calms down and maintains her Surge. I notice that while her wings are still visible, the rest of her Surge is at an even temper.

After a moment to process everything, she speaks about her goals.

"I will do my best, father. Somehow, I've always known there was something else in my body due to my subconscious thoughts and dreams, but I was never sure. When I was young, I wondered about those bursts of energy. Now I know."

I ponder and compile all the information from Lucius.

"So, then this explains my powers, the Regiment, and why The Conduit exists. We don't know who created it, but I'm sure it was people related to the Seraphs. Or maybe the original Seraphs. No wonder Lucius kept it so secret. If this information or you fell into the military's hands..."

Josephine does not hear my analysis. She is undergoing her own.

"We won't worry about that Afia. This power. It's like every piece of technology in Accra is available to me. I can even sense some other seraphs. Afia is this what it's like? To truly understand the Surge."

I smile at her discovery.

"Nowhere near that level."

She pauses during her self-assessment.

"Wait. There are several military units headed our way."

I open my mouth in surprise.

"Why now? How are they here?!"

I tap into my frequency for another attempt to reach Abeem. At first there is only silence and static.

Then a voice with no emotion comes on.

"This is Abeem..."

I sigh in relief of her voice.

"Abeem! Thank the Orishas you're ok. Do you know why there is a military presence headed my way?"

She hesitates then answers.

"Afia, I'm so sorry to do this. The military needs the Conduit. There is a lot of good we could do with it. The military even

offered to fully support my family. And as much as I care about you, my family matters more."

I listen for a while. Then I turn off my frequency in anger. I seethe in my anger at Abeem's betrayal. Then I think it's only fair for me to leave her years ago.

I move to tell Josephine.
"Josephine, we've got to move immediately."
She suggests an option.
"Take me to the shore. We should be safe there." I think about how far the Cape Coast is.
"But that's a few miles away. And how would you even know that?"
She silences my fears with confidence in her Surge powers.
"The Surge is calling me there. My powers seem to be focused on that point. Just trust me."

End Chapter 30

****

Chapter 31

We speed out towards the coast. I can still hear military alarms going off behind us. We weave through the city of Accra, dodging the military and military police. The military trucks shoot their vibro-guns at us. I accelerate more to keep my distance. In my rearview mirror, I see Abeem driving one of the closest trucks. She launches a Surge-dampening net toward my car. I open a window and fire off a Surge blast at it. The net and my blast hit each other and explode.

I curse at Abeem under my breath.
"Damn you Abeem for being true to yourself instead of being true to me! I know you have a family but still." I see Josephine *in the backseat with her eyes closed and calm.* "Josephine, *here! Grab this gun! See if you can...hey...Josephine?"*

I try to hand her my gun, but she's in a seraphic trance. I continue to maneuver away from the gunfire as best I can. Eventually, I hear the sound of a military helicopter overhead. Once the helicopter is in position it shoots rockets at us. Before those rockets can even reach us, time stands still. An angelic glow engulfs the helicopter, the trucks and me. Every piece of technology in its radius stalls out. The trucks smash together and the helicopter falls from the sky. I get out of my car to see that its roof is wide open. I crane my neck at the culprit of the hole. It is Josephine, who hovers over the ground with the Surge swirling around her barely perceivable outline as a Seraph. Her aura surrounds and projects into all of the technology nearby.

She watches my confusion.
"Don't worry Afia. We are still able to go to the Cape Coast. There is nowhere we can't go now. We don't need the car."

Before I can react, she picks me up and glides towards the Cape Coast. The military sits dumbfounded and tries to mobilize their troops. However, Josephine and I are history in a blaze of blue light. We cross over fields of green and trees. The green turns brown as the Atlantic Ocean comes into view. Eventually, we find a small beach area on the Cape Coast to settle.

I catch my breath. Then I explain to Josephine why all's not well.

"The military won't stop Josephine. General Aku in Kumasi is no joke. She would do anything to see the Asante Kingdom overtake all of Ghana. The Accra military is bad enough. And hell, if I know Abeem and her mission to support her family, I know she won't stop either."

She explains her thinking with tranquility.

"The issues with Abeem will have to be something you reconcile on your own. However, the military won't be dealing with us for now. With my power, it was impossible to trace us. Afia, thank you for all that you've done. My father's safe money has been transferred to you minus the Sirius cut already. I'm going to go back to the origin of the Surge to see if I can find other Seraphs."

The confidence of Josephine is refreshing. I ask some of my last questions.

"That's why you took us to this beach, correct? It's the edge of Ghana. Where we need to be for the Surge."

She agrees and adds more ideas.

"Yes, but I also took us here to unlock your potential with the Surge."

The Conduit glows in Josephine's hand. She touches it to my temple. Shockwaves are sent through my body. It feels like my spine realigns and my body renews again with Surge.

She tells me of my new powers.
"You are no Seraph Afia, but you now have much more control of your powers than you ever did. Safeguard the Conduit with your life. Perhaps one day you can join us in the ether, but I know you've got more to do in Ghana. I wish you the best."

With a wave of angelic electricity, Josephine rises into the air. She coasts over the ocean. I wonder what I can do with my new Surge powers. With the Conduit, I soon realize I can cloak myself to scans and my blasts are significantly stronger. I marvel at my progress and head off towards the Cape Coast. Hopefully I can find a village to lay low in.

My holopad chimes. I check the message.
"Sirius thanks you for your cooperation. We have sent the remaining amount from our deal to your online account."

I trace my credits at 4,000,000 richer. I smile and enjoy the gorgeous coast at sundown.

End Chapter 31

****

Epilogue to Pulse of the City

A frequency from General Aku calls in. A stern, but light voice speaks.

"Major Abeem, I thought you were able to track Afia and the Seraph."

Abeem explains the situation.

"Yes, General Aku, but they seem to have vanished."

General Aku laughs and wonders.

"I mean what? Did the shockhead go into the ocean?

Abeem disagrees and gives more details.

"No, her, the Seraph and the Conduit appear to have gone to the Cape Coast. Afterwards, we lost all tracking information on them."

General Aku focuses on this news. She then speaks with excitement.

"Report to Kumasi base Major Abeem. We will discuss next steps here. We have improvements to our Surge-dampening systems now.   Come join me in bringing the Asante Kingdom back to its former glory."

Abeem replies with affirmation.

"Yes, General Aku."

She silently says a mantra to herself.

"Afia, this isn't over, I will find you."

End of Epilogue to Part 3

****

Chapter 32 - Insurgent Code (Part 4)

Cape Coast 4 Months Later

It's strange to not be in a major city. I, Afia Osuwu, keep to myself. I don't talk to the CDA or the military. I simply fish and return to my hut like my ancestors used to. I enjoy drinking palm wine with local fisherpeople while we watch the tide roll in. We rest easy under the setting sun until our eyes feel heavy. The sea breeze carries the scent of fish. Ever since the Surge, there are far less cruisers these days. Thus the fish population increases throughout the coast. I know no one in the village complaints about that boon. Today, I'm going to fish in a new boat. I take my new net too in order to hopefully get a good haul for trade. The village doesn't use credits. Everything is on a pre-Surge barter system. I like it this way.

My old neighbor greets me on my way to the coast.
"Ey Afia, going to get a good haul?"
I respond in kind.
"You know it. How's the tide?"
He tells me his prediction.
"She just started rising this morning."

I watch the other villagers set out on their boats to fish with their families. That beautiful West African sun sets over the horizon and warms my back as I head out to sea. The high tide brings in all kinds of fish into my net. I relax lazily after a couple of hauls and drift off to sleep. After a couple hours, my Surge powers stir me awake. I am not actively using my powers so I don't know how I can feel them.

Then a voice appears in my mind.
<Afia...Afia...>

My first thought is that it is Lacuna, back from the dead.
<Lacuna? Impossible...> I recognize the voice more clearly.
<Josephine?>

She continues her telepathic Surge outreach.
<Afia don't be alarmed. I need your help>

I don't understand her request.
<How?! Why would you even need my help? You're basically a Goddess now.>

She focuses me to get serious.
<Afia, the military has developed technology to hinder Seraphs. They used the archives in Accra and the research from Abeem. These Surge dampeners are the most powerful General Aku has produced>

I freeze at the horrifying revelation.
<Wait more powerful than the old ones?>

She continues her explanation.
<Yes Afia, they can launch the dampeners now. And their strength is much stronger. They caught me while researching the Kumasi slums for traces of a possible Seraph.>

I tell her my concern for her well-being.
<That's not good at all Josephine. Where are you?>

She reveals her location and much more.
<In a military cell in Kumasi. There are other people with Surge here. They're siphoning our powers to help create pure Surge energy. They're using the Conduit to enhance this process. They might create another Singularity if they're not careful. General Aku and the Chief Doctor Boateng plan to experiment with my power for their weapons. I think they're also trying to use the dampeners on some of those Regiment types as well.>

I wonder about her line about the Regiment.
<The Regiment is in Kumasi too? Is there no way to fight this power?"

She explains that there isn't.

Josephine's voice dissipates in my head. I am struck with confusion and anxiety in the middle of the sea with my net floating away. Some of the villagers come over when they see me panic. I quickly row to shore and go to my hut. I gather my credit chip, my vibro-blaster, fresh clothes and the keys to a car I stole a month ago. If I'm going to Kumasi, hopefully my brother, Kwaku, can help. I only hope he's willing to see me.

End Chapter 32

****

Chapter 33

Kumasi - Home of the powerful Asante Kingdom.

The drive to Kumasi is thankfully uneventful. Back on the main roads, I use vigilance to look out for any military police who may be searching for me. I can dock my car in a private parking lot. I pay the valet a few credits on the side to keep quiet about my appearance. No doubt there are military scanners and checkpoints present. However, maybe the military is calm after their recent captures of Seraphs and Surge candidates.

I walk into Kumasi and recall my memories of the kingdom. The Asante Kingdom is a kingdom without conquerors. They are probably the most powerful kingdom in West Africa. Only the Fulani Coalition from Nigeria rivals them. This is mainly in part to the efforts of General Aku's mother, Admiral Aku. Now, General Aku rules Kumasi with totalitarian authority. She is a ruthless woman who actively discriminates against Surge users, the gangs and the lower class. Thus, where Accra is filled with neon and fun, Kumasi is a heartless shell of cold steel military buildings everywhere except for the lower class slums.

My only hope is to avoid her. I know too many stories about her confrontations with Lacuna. I shudder at the thought and remember my purpose. I think my brother, Kwaku, still works at the Kwame Nkrumah University as a professor. So many retired military people do that. I think to myself about how I did not contact him in the past. It does not please me. I check the registry at the university and see that he is still a professor there. I cloak myself and make my way to his office. I cloak out and knock on his door.

My brother's voice responds to the knock
"Office hours are from 1-3pm today, please come back later."

I push to talk to him.
"It's urgent!"
I can hear his footsteps come to the door.
"I haven't heard that voice in years. Afia?!"

He quickly opens the door and I'm face to face with a machete.

I back away from him.
"Put that down brother."
He yells in anger from the past.
"No, not until you state your reasoning, you will not take anything or hurt me ever again!"
I wish I could update him on my progress.
"I've long since left the Harvesters Kwaku. I'm a detective in Accra."

I remember that I still have my CDA certification on me. I show it to him.

He is still incredulous of me.
"You could've stolen that. Why the hell should I trust you and what do you want from me?"
I will attempt to explain my situation.
"I need your help for something really important. I know you know I have The Surge powers, but the rest, you're going to have to sit down to hear."
He is stubborn to my plea.
"I don't want to."
I beg him to forget about his issues with me.
"Kwaku, please. I have a friend in danger, and I know you can help. You and me can solve issues later. But this person is in need."
He relents to me a little.

"Alright, I'll see your holopad with whatever you have going on. But Afia, I swear on Shango, if you screw up even once…We're done. And know that I still don't trust you"

I hand him my holopad.

"It's a start."

The holopad shows him most of my CDA life, the chase for the Conduit and the information on Josephine. After updating him on everything, he stares into space for a long time.

He finally speaks.

"If it wasn't for your holopad I wouldn't believe a word of this. All this time in the CDA and you never said hello. You never checked on Baba and Mama. You couldn't even go to the funeral?!"

The memory saddens me.

"I talked to them at least once before they went. They were still mad, but they were happy to see me."

He ponders my comment.

"Wonder why they didn't tell me."

I tell him about himself.

"Look at your reaction? Do you think they could've told you? Or I could've gone to the funeral? Even as a detective, I wasn't welcome in Kumasi. You didn't even believe I left the Harvesters."

He sits down at his desk and sighs.

"Fine Afia. I wish things had been better. They grieved so much when you were gone."

I sit in the chair across from him.

"I know, brother. But now I need your help. Perhaps in time we can reconnect."

He smiles for a moment.

"It's good to have family again even if I'm skeptical. So you say Josephine is in the military stronghold? But you already know it can't be breached. You have no army and General Aku is the fiercest around. What will you do?"

I bite my lip and think.

"You don't know of anyone or anything?"

He brainstorms with me for a moment.

"Sirius probably knows all. Wait, actually, there is an old ex-Harvester who is extremely skilled with tech. She runs a shop for both the military and civilians. It's in Kejetia Market. As a matter of fact, you might know her. She uses Mama and Baba's healing arm technology."

I can't believe what he is saying. There's no way Xochitl could be up here.

"An ex-Harvester skilled in tech? Someone who knows how to use those blueprints. Hmmm, I might know them. There's a handful of Harvesters who left when the boss, Machado, left."

He continues to describe her.

"She came here a while back. I talked with her a couple of times. Goes by the name of Xochitl."

I knock over my chair when I stand up immediately.

"Xochitl's alive?!"

My brother looks at me in equal surprise.

"You know her?!

I orient the chair and sit. Some sense of happiness comes to me.

"Absolutely brother. She's one of the only people that rode for me in that gang when everything went south. I haven't seen her since I joined the academy."

He gathers his things and sprints to the door.

"Let's go see her then."

I join him swiftly.

"Yes, let's! We'll have to figure out later about the army. Unless there are more Surge members here?"

A melancholic expression comes across his phase.

"Yeah, but the General is a tyrant! All people of the Surge, especially the poor, are collared. And that doctor Boateng is just as bad. They often experiment on Surge candidates. But come, these things must not be said inside university walls."

End of Chapter 33

<u>Chapter 34</u>

Kejetia Market.

Miraculously, the Asante military let the market still be a place of life amongst the oppressive empire. It's possible because General Aku prefers shopping for Kente cloth here. She allows neon billboards to still show shopkeepers names and wares. Hell, you might even find some pre-Surge music and electronics here as well. Even if they're bootleg items from the black market, any joy is a nice little revolt against the General. Everyone partakes in the hustle and bustle here, but I notice a few people with collars begging for credits. We finally reach Xochitl's repair shop. Pieces of tech clutter the entire shop. Xochitl scrutinizes a computer. She retains all of her tattoos, but wears less piercings. I also notice her shorter hair. As such, it's good to see she still takes care of herself.

Kwaku walks over to talk to her first.
"Hey there Xochitl. How goes it?"
She responds in kind.
"It's ok Kwaku. The military is paying me top dollar for working with this new output of Surge. It looks vaguely familiar, but the property seems different. I've been trying to figure out how to make the power tempered enough for individual use. "
He leans in with more interest.
"Really? Do you know what they want to do with it?"
She shrugs and picks up another piece of tech.
"Maybe dampeners, maybe new weapons. Either way it's not for something positive. It's blood money, but money never flows free anymore thanks to the General."
I notice that the two of them are flirting. Once I do, Xochitl locks eyes with me.
"Hey there, I..say I think I know you. Mierda! Afia?!"

I run over to hug her tight.

"Xochitl!! It's so good to see you again. It's been what? a decade?"

She holds me a little longer.

"I think so, I haven't seen you since Accra. I tried to come back with medical help, but you were long gone."

I recall the day.

"The military patched me up and hired me. I've been with the CDA all this time. "

She then wonders why I'm in Kumasi.

"What the hell are you doing here? Does this mean you're not a Harvester anymore either?"

I nod in agreement.

"Haven't been in years, but I need that tech help of yours."

She throws her hands up away from the situation.

"Hey, I said money was tight, but I'm not starting up a new gang."

I reassure her for a moment.

"Remember, I'm not a Harvester. I'm a detective and I need your skills to get into the military stronghold."

My suggestion surprises her even more.

"Are you trying to rob the golden stool? That's one of the dumbest things you could do. If you're a detective, then que demonio para fortress?

I try to show her my holopad.

"No, just listen, Xochitl. I'm trying to rescue someone in there. With my holopad it will-"

Before I can continue, I sense a faint Surge presence and some high-grade military technology nearby. I can make out the trace appearance of a military official. I immediately cloak myself and move to the back of Xochitl's shop.

Xochitl searches around in confusion.

"Wait, que infierno? She was just here."

Kwaku placates her.
"I think she told me she has these powers. She said they're from some Conduit. It's probably better if she tells you."
She now consoles him.
"You mean the Surge? I knew about that. But this is brand new, whatever it is."

At that moment, General Aku, the leader of the Asante Kingdom and Kumasi enters the shop. She is a blonde, copper-skinned, tall, and fitness-muscled lady in full military regalia. Behind her, follows the bald, short, tattooed, and fidgeting Chief Doctor Boateng.

General Aku introduces herself with an air of menace.
"Hey Xochitl, how goes it? O and hello Professor Kwaku. What brings you here to this shop?"
My brother responds with nervousness.
"Simply trying to get some generator parts."
The general nods slowly and moves to Xochitl.
"Understandable. How are the dampeners? And the new weapon conductors"
Xochitl responds while looking down. She never looks away from people.
"Dampeners are doing well. I'm making some progress with the weapons and might be able to have at least a pistol."
Dr. Boateng sniffs the air.
"I smell the Surge…ah that's where it's coming from. O look, an ungrateful shockhead peasant."

I realize that the doctor can smell the Surge. I hold my breath, but then see a sickly person with a Surge dampener collar on them. Dr. Boateng and General Aku eye them maliciously.

The sickly person enters Xochitl's shop. They don't know the general until it's too late.
"Hey Xochitl, were you able to get...O damn the Orishas, please no General Aku."
The general responds to them.
"The Orishas? You must be from Nigeria, Boateng is from there as well. I miss that culture. Maybe you're new to the city too. That might be why you thought to bring it up to an officer of the Asante Kingdom. You know that I'm the only Goddess you need."

She strides up to the unknown victim and grabs them by the collar. She shakes them to their knees and brings out a staff. She presses a button on the staff that signals the dampener to shock the victim at the neck. She then proceeds to whack the victim in the back of the knees to make them kneel. Xochitl and Kwaku watch anxiously while Doctor Boateng beams with glee.

The general continues her onslaught verbally.
"You should know to always be on your knees in front of the general, shockhead maggot... I should kill you where you stand. However, I don't want blood in Xochitl's shop. Hmm. I know. I'll let Dr. Boateng take you back for fun. We always need more of the Surge. Is that ok with you Doc?"
The doctor raises their nose with delight.
"A Nigerian shockhead, this is most intriguing. They must be the reason I smell so much Surge."

Sweat trickles down my brow. I watch the scene in silent fear. These two are a menace.
The general drags the victim away. Dr. Boateng follows her.

As she leaves, General Aku imparts a message.

"Keep up with those dampeners Xochitl. We'll come to collect the new weapons at the end of the week. I trust everything will be ready by then." She then addresses my brother. *"Kwaku, good seeing you. Since you're military university personnel, I hope you let us know next time you need Xochitl's tech. Glory to the Golden Stool!"*

Xochitl and Kwaku reply in unified fear.
"Glory to the Golden Stool!"

When they leave, I disengage my cloak. I need a moment to catch my breath.

Once I am able, I ask Xochitl about the general.
"That's General Aku?! Xochitl, how can you help her and make money off of those slave collars?!"

She ignores my caution.
"What the hell other choice do I have?! She's the general of the Asante military! I'm not going back to harvesting. This is all I have."

I reason with her.
"Damn Xochitl. We have our work cut out for us if we want to beat her. Now let me explain what is going on."

I finally show my holopad of all the events involving Josephine to her.

She sits down to process everything.
"Damn puta, that's a hell of a story. And that holopad proves it. Come to the backroom. I have layouts of all the government buildings here."

My brother wonders about her resourcefulness.
"How did you manage to get those blueprints?"

She explains her good fortune.
"Working to improve tech for the military also requires knowing where to put defensive weapons. The military gave me a blueprint for all of their primary buildings."

We examine Xochitl's blueprints of the Asante stronghold – the hologram technology shows access points, general security and guard shifts.

Xochitl tells some strategies.
"The underground bunker is our best bet, especially since I can get us in as cargo for a routine pickup."
My brother questions her motives.
"Hold on. You're ready to suddenly help us and leave your job."
She laughs at his question.
"Pinche cabron. I love fucking with the military. I have no allegiance to them. Helping an old friend is better than gold. And it will be good to rescue the seraph. Honestly though, I'll grab some military-grade tech for profit too. It will be like old Harvesting times."
He shakes his head.
"I knew it."
However, I agree with her wholeheartedly.
"Yeah, it's just like harvesting a warehouse. I'm here for it."
Kwaku is still skeptical of the situation.
"That's great and all but we still have no army and no guns."
Xochitl gives some solutions.
"I have a Sirius contact who could probably help us with the guns. As for an army... I need to show you the market slums. There's a lot of lower-class Surge people hiding out from General Aku there. Some don't even have dampeners on them."
I pace around the shop with her solutions on my brain.
"So if we grab guns from Sirius and get the Surge people as army we could be set."
My brother puts my plan into perspective.
"I'm willing to believe those guns will require a military raid. How are we going to do that alone? Then we'll have to use

that to convince the people in the slums to fight. This is going to be tough."

Xochitl puts up a hand to pause him.
"I'll call Sirius, they'll know what's up."

Xochitl turns on her holovid to call.

The screen buzzes. Soon a member of Sirius appears on the transmitter.
"This is Sirius."

I see that it is a random member of Sirius as always. They remain anonymous. I wonder if they know about my previous run-ins with them.

Xochitl greets Sirius in a cheerful manner.
"Good to see you again Sirius. I need some military-grade weapons. Any way to find a surplus in Kumasi?"
They contemplate her request.
"We do, but it will be very costly. Wait, is that the fugitive Afia with you? We have heard of your movements in Accra before leaving the detective agency. The credits we gave her will suffice for this cost. Come to the outpost on the edge of the Kejetia Market and the rainforest."
My brother smirks at me.
"Afia, I'll have to hear more of these stories eventually. I see you left out some details of your extracurriculars."
I smile with embarrassment.
"It was a hell of a time."

Xochitl snaps at us and tells us to get a move on.

End Chapter 34
****

Chapter 35

We head towards the outpost. As we near, Xochitl remarks that we can take the weapons right to the slums since they're close to the outpost. Plus, no one cares what you bring in. The hard part will be getting people with the Surge out. We reach an abandoned shipping area that seems to be an old military transit stop. We walk to the front door of the outpost and it opens.

We hear a voice speak.
"Sirius welcomes you."

When we enter, we realize that a different member of Sirius than on the holovid greets us.

They ask about payment.
"I trust you have the credits."
I motion to my holopad.
"Right here. But first, where are the guns?"
They send us to the back of the outpost.
"Just wait in the back."

As we stroll to the back, a military truck arrives outside.

An Asante soldier starts a dialogue with the Sirius member.
"Hey brother, is the shipment here?"
They respond with extra information.
"Yes, and so is your bounty. This is off the record, correct?"
The bounty hunter agrees with them.
"Correct, so therefore I won't be needing you anymore."
They put their hands up. They give a cautionary glance to the bounty hunter.
"You would betray Sirius?"
The bounty hunter looms larger than he is.

"Yes, I am Sirius. How does it feel to be double-crossed for once in your life? It's only fair since you betrayed the people of the Surge."

He unholsters a vibro-gun. I send a wave of Surge to his gun. He shoots the Sirius member in the stomach. He notices us. Before he can react, I quickly lockdown his military armor electronics to freeze him in place. We disarm him right after.

Xochitl shakes the Sirius member. She wants information before they bleed out.
"Sirius, where's the guns!?"
They weakly point to the truck.
"In the truck. You do know you must kill him before the military finds out?"
I wave off their threat.
"We can simply leave him locked here without his armor to give off a signal. Sirius, this lowers our deal. Why would you betray us?"
They state nonchalantly.
"It's the military. Unfortunately, they are almost always the highest bidder. Especially compared to the gangs."
I shrug and acknowledge their statement.
"Fair but you're only getting half."
They nod their head.
"Sirius knows this and…"

The Sirius member bleeds out unconscious. In order to make sure the deal goes through; I scan my credit chip to upload to Sirius. We put the military bounty hunter in the back of the outpost. We then remove his electronic military armor. Xochitl uses her tech to start the truck engine.

I pick up the armor and size up my brother.
"Hey Kwaku, you think this armor might fit you?"
He moves away from me.

"Why would I wear that?"

I tell him what I'm thinking.

"It can help us infiltrate anywhere. It's military-grade even if that bounty hunter was probably not even military."

He adds on to my plan.

"Should we question him?"

I disagree and give him the armor.

"Nah. But try it on. It probably fits and will be helpful."

Xochitl interrupts our scheming.

"Come on people! We don't have the time. No point in questioning him. He's probably just a Cloak looking to score."

Kwaku climbs into the truck with the armor.

"Alright I'll see how this fits as we go."

While I worry about the recent betrayal, I hop in the back of the truck. When I get in, I see all the military guns. Even if the military knows we are here, we'll be ready. Then, Xochitl speeds off in the direction of the slums.

End Chapter 35

****

Chapter 36

We park the truck outside of the slums. Kwaku puts on the military uniform. He pretends to supervise us at the slums' checkpoint. We see a long line of people waiting to get out of the slums. The guards are doing a thorough body scan inspection of everyone and their belongings. I grit my teeth. It will be difficult to get anything out of here. Kwaku waves Xochitl and I through the checkpoint. He does the gesture in view of the military guards so they know we're with him. He bids us farewell and goes back to prepare for our escape.

I survey the slums. The interlocking pathways and slipshod buildings create a jumble of green, black and gold color schemes. The colors of the Asante empire. The banners and awnings create an interwoven web of confusion. The smells of years of stagnation reek from the impoverished dwellings. The heat is stronger here. There is no weather control in this region of Kumasi. While all of these elements keep the slums firmly in the lower class, there is still joy in the air. Children squabble and play throughout the buildings. A group of people celebrate around a makeshift bonfire. For all that General Aku oppresses, the will of people marches on.

After taking everything in, I ask Xochitl about our direction.
"Alright Xochitl, where are we going in this labyrinth?"
She responds with an idea.
"We need to grab a guide. They'll help us deal with this complicated maze."

I breathe a sigh of relief. The labyrinth of alleyways is already confusing from the outside. I catch up with Xochitl as she finds us a guide.

She finds a bystander near the entrance to the slums.

"Hola amigo! We are looking for some people who have some, ah, extra Surge."

The guide dismisses her.

"I know not what you are talking about. However, if you need a guide to our markets or food carts I can help."

To help his persuasion, I show him a bit of Surge electricity in my hands.

"I think you know what we need."

The guide steps back in awe.

"You have The Surge?!" He rushes to hide my hands. *"Keep that on the low. Anyways, come, the Regiment is waiting for you."*

To my surprise, the Regiment is present in Kumasi as well.

"The Regiment is here?! How is that even possible?!"

The guide assuages my confusion.

"Only a small faction. You know the group in Accra. The Regiment has ties and allies everywhere. Here we are small because of the General. But we are still mighty."

While he talks, we walk up and down the slums. The path winds forever until we reach a tarp. The guide lifts the tarp, revealing a staircase going down. We head down and encounter some slum dwellers. Some are wearing Surge dampeners. The lighting is low, but I can see the traces of purple and white in the slum dwellers' clothing. It is emblematic of the Regiment.

The guide announces our entrance.

"Nao, we have new Surge people! They're not the Regiment, but they seem powerful."

An older Regiment member, with a broken dampener, steps up. Her name is Nao. She is of good height, dark skin with several wrinkles, very slim and a head full of gray locs.

Her and other Regiment members wear purple and white hooded robes. Not all of them are Regiment though. A handful of slum-dwellers sit with the Regiment.

The elder, Nao, questions our presence.
"What brings you here? We saw from the guide's recording that you do have the power. So hopefully you are not some new military invention they've sent to betray us."
I wonder at the mention of invention. Still, I set their fears at ease.
"I am not here from that crazy lady, General Aku. However, like you, I have the Surge. I have slightly more power due to this right here. This is the Conduit, and I will explain not only how it works but why I need your help in getting it back."

I show them my holovid to explain my time in Accra. I also show all of them what the Conduit is and how it can amplify their powers. Xochitl adds in about the issues in Kumasi. I hope they will join me. Saving Josephine and the Conduit, liberating themselves and stopping the military are all things I know we can accomplish together.

Nao ponders my offering.
"Will any of this actually be possible?"
I encourage her with more support.
"It can be. We must use the Surge correctly. We've also got guns from a military shipment. Also, we can use my brother's house on the outskirts to regroup."
She agrees but asks how to get past the checkpoint.
"How do we get past the checkpoint? Even with the Surge they'll stop my gang and the slum-dwellers swiftly."
I think hard about it. I suggest an idea even if it's risky.
"I can power it down, so we won't be scanned. However, that will signify the military. As such, we're going to need the slum-dwellers' help. You'll have to rush them in the confusion."

The slum-dwellers hesitate then nod in spite of their worry.
"I hope they are only arrested. We'll need the diversion to get The Regiment and Surge candidates out."
Nao takes a breath. She joins our cause with caution.
"We believe in your fight, but we will have to move fast after we regroup. General Aku and the guards will take this attack lightly."
I thank her excessively.
"Thank the Orishas! I appreciate this more than you know."
She addresses her people.
"Alright listen up everyone! We now have the power to use our Surge in order to finally move out of here. Some of you without the Surge are going to have to help us. No matter what happens, we will honor you to the Orishas. The choice is yours. You may leave if you feel safer. I cannot force you to risk your lives for the sake of our freedom."

There is silence in the underground chamber. Not a soul leaves the room.

The guide rallies behind Nao.
"We've been oppressed long enough Nao. Damn General Aku and Damn the Asante Kingdom. We'll do whatever it takes. "
Nao raises her first.
"It's settled then. Let's go!"

With a roar of approval from the underground hideout, The Regiment and the slum-dwellers march out. I transfer some power the Surge candidates. This enables them to shut any remaining Surge dampeners down. We navigate as quickly as we can through the winding architecture of the slums. The guide directs me to military generators for the checkpoint's electricity. As I get closer, I notice a familiar face watching over the guards…Abeem! Millions of questions cross my mind. Why is she here? Is she helping Aku learn about the Surge? Family over everything, right Abeem? I shake off my anxiety over my scattered thoughts. I turn my focus to the mission and power down the generators with my Surge.

Several guards run around trying to figure out why the power is down.
"What the hell is going on with our power?!"
Abeem interjects with commands.
"Private, get that power back on right now! We can't afford to have the checkpoint down."

After her statement, the slum-dwellers and the Regiment rush the guards. The guards try to defend against the fists, sticks and rocks of the slum-dwellers. Next, Nao channels her and the main Regiment's Surge to create a barrier. It helps them move through the checkpoint with protection. They move in every direction as they spill out of the slums. Nao, Xochitl and some others run back to the truck. The guards try to corral the slum-dwellers.

Abeem reports the chaos to Aku.
"General, we've got a situation here. The slums are going wild and our power is down."
She immediately sends troops.
"I'm sending a force right now. Major, hold them off. You may use dampeners and lethal force."
Abeem complies with her command.
"Yes. General. Guards, lethal force and dampeners are approved!"

The guards open fire on the escapees. Several people go down. Dampeners fly out to capture some of the Regiment. A few slum-dwellers have vibro-guns. The slums decay into a war zone. I continue to watch the chaos while keeping an eye on Abeem. Before I leave, I see a slum-dweller rush at

Abeem's back. I stun them with a Surge blast. Abeem looks around for the origin of the blast. I cloak myself and sprint to the truck and my brother.

Not finding the origin of the blast, Abeem's confusion rises.
"Afia? Was that you just now? No. It was probably just another Surge person. Why would they save me though…"
Gunshots continue to crack loudly into the sky from the battle. I see Kwaku in his military uniform. He ushers several people onto the truck. He sees me and comes to my aid.

I tell him to start the truck.
"Kwaku I'm fine, get the truck started before the military gets here."
He stares behind me. Several military guards are closing in.
"O shit! Alright, I'm on it."
I hop on the truck with Nao, Xochitl and more Regiment.
"Faster Kwaku! Get that truck going now."

A few slum-dwellers try to escape to us, but die from the military gunfire at their backs. As we speed off, I see Abeem call her guards back. She does not want to pursue us. I still don't know what she is thinking, but I am grateful for her mercy.

End Chapter 36
****

Chapter 37

We arrive at my brother's spacious home. Its layout reminds me of my parents' home. This is all possible because he is a high-ranking university employee. He even keeps sculptures and tribal masks from our family home. However, there is no time to admire his abode.

I gather all of the allies into the main living room. *"Alright, everyone, it won't be long before the military tracks our whereabouts. We've got to move into the next phase right away. The Regiment and slum-dwellers will take on the military stronghold on its weaker side entrances. The military guns will help with this, but the military will even pool their forces there. Be ready for anything. Xochitl will support you all with her tech. I'll be infiltrating the stronghold through this hatch. While they're distracted with the battle, I'll be able to find Josephine and the Conduit."*

Xochitl elaborates on her job further. *"I'm going to set fire to my shop. No sense in helping the military anymore. When I do, I'll grab my spare tech to support the main assault."*

Nao tells her people what to do. *"We're going to use the vibro-rifles from the shipment. Regiment we will unite our Surge powers to have a fighting chance against the military.*

Kwaku announces his plan. *"Afia, I'm going with you."*

I'm happy he wishes to accompany me, but I warn him. *"Kwaku, it's much too dangerous to infiltrate. I can handle myself."*

He remains stubborn about the situation. *"You don't know what anti-Surge powers they have. If your powerful friend was able to be captured, you could be too."*

I consider what he says. Eventually, I relent and ask for his help. It will be good to fight alongside my brother.

I address everyone, one final time.
"Everyone listen up. While this is a long way from my days as a detective, we have a chance to liberate Kumasi and put an end to General Aku's reign. Let's follow the plan. Let's become free."

There is a resounding cheer while everyone begins preparations. Nao drives off with the truck and her people to the stronghold. Xochitl rides with them to get to her shop for the first diversion. Kwaku and I prepare for our rescue mission. I will most likely face Abeem. I'm not sure what I will say to her. I don't know how she will feel about me, but perhaps I can help her see reason one last time.

End Chapter 37

****

Chapter 38

From the distance, we see smoke rise from Xochitl's shop. This is our signal to move to attack the stronghold. We hear on Kwaku's military radio that there is a squad investigating the smoke. With our distraction in full effect, the guards may be lighter at the side gates. We approach the front gates of the stronghold first. They display a large Golden Stool, the symbol of the Asante military. We pivot to one of the side gates. Our predictions are correct in that there are less guards on this side. Nao and the Regiment begin their Surge attack, while Kwaku and I move to a hatch nearby.

Nao rallies her people with a battle cry.
"Alright everyone, hit them with everything you got!!"

The Regiment powers down the stronghold side gate. Slum-dwellers pour into the side entrance. They throw bombs and shoot vibro-rifles at several structures. Then they switch their targets to soldiers as the military rush to the side entrance. I hope that The Regiment can outlast the military. Their anti-personnel guns and cyber shields are difficult to contend with. While that chaos is happening, Kwaku and I make our way down to the underground of the stronghold. I shut off the cameras. We open Xochitl's blueprints and follow them to Josephine's cell. Kwaku sets explosive charges while we move through it. He says he wants to bring down the stronghold once we leave. I agree with him and feel out for Josephine's Surge pulses. We occasionally duck into a corridor whenever the military runs past to the outside battle. Eventually we find Josephine's holding cell. There is another Seraph nearby, but they are already dead.

I exclaim my excitement upon seeing her.

"Josephine! Thank the Orishas. It is so good to see you again."

A weak Josephine calls out to me.

"Afia? Is that you? You made it! I'm sorry I couldn't reach out for more details, but my power had already begun to wane. Who is this?"

My brother introduces himself.

"I'm Afia's brother, Kwaku. You must be Josephine?"

She greets him. Then she tells us everything.

"Yes. You came just in time, Afia. The military has already started to drain Seraph power for their weapons. My fellow mate here, Twaino, has already produced new weapons using his seraphic energy. There is no time to mourn though. Dr. Boateng could be back any moment."

I ask about her capture.

"How did they capture you? I see the dampeners but how? Seraphs are too strong for those."

To my dismay, she tells us about a sinister weapon.

"They have a limited use wave motion gun that nullifies all Surge. Also, I wasn't in my seraphic state while searching Kumasi for Twaino. He and I were simply civilians. If you didn't know our Surge trace, you wouldn't know we had it."

I release Josephine from her draining cell. I prop her up to leave.. Kwaku sets a charge in the lab area. Before we exit, we hear a raspy voice and the hum of a vibro-gun behind us.

Dr. Boateng commands us in their signature rasp.

"Put the Seraph back. I can't allow you to go further."

Josephine pleads for them to reconsider.

"Dr. please you have gotten all you can from us. I could give you more knowledge if you let me return to my Seraphs."

They disagree and step closer.

"That is unlikely. Hmm your friend must be a Seraph too. Her odor of The Surge is strong. Seems familiar. The market..."

Kwaku questions their awareness.

"How can you sense them?!"

The doctor conveys their past to us.

"You see, I once had The Surge too. I learned and experimented on myself to surgically remove it. As I did with the rest of my body in becoming a man."

I cannot believe they have the power to sense Surge in that way.

"How is that even possible?"

The doctor mulls it over. They decide not to explain.

"I could tell you, but that would take far too long. Also, I have no desire to hand over my personal secret... Enough talk."

Before Dr. Boateng can shoot, I release Surge sparks in their direction. They absorb the sparks in a special shield. They come closer to us. I see my brother notice how close they are to the bomb charge he left in the lab.

They gloat over their victory.

"Dear, I have done enough research to know you are powerless against..."

Kwaku sets off his charge and a loud boom echoes through the lab. It blows up in Dr. Boateng's face and pushes us back across the lab. After a moment of disorientation, I can make out an angelic glow. Josephine's seraphic powers blocked us from being hit by the bomb. However, the glow is fading. It's one of her last remnants of power.

I yell to my brother.

"Kwaku! Josephine is fading fast. We gotta go. How many more charges have you got?"

He gets up from the ground.

"Hell of a blast, ugh. But as soon as I set this one I'm done. The rest are on timers. So we need to keep moving. If you want me to detonate them earlier, say the word."

I hurry him along.

"Cool, set your last charges and let's get outta here. Help me with Josephine. According to the blueprints, we can go out the other side entrance. I hear the gunfire, the military is still distracted. We should be good to go."

We push towards the other side entrance. There appears to be no troops in our way.

However, when we pass the military training arena, Abeem shouts at us to stop.

"Afia! Stop this instant and get in here!"

I turn to her then beg her to listen.

"Why the hell are you still helping them, Abeem?!"

She looks down and does not make eye contact.

"The military keeps my family alive; you know this. I'm sorry but I have to stop you. General Aku wouldn't tolerate any less."

I glance at Josephine. Then, I offer an option to Abeem.

"Then let's fight for it like we used to, passionately. No Surge and no military equipment."

She puts down her military weapons and gear.

"That's fair, Afia. You know how much I don't want to do this."

I laugh and call her.

"But duty calls, ey Abeem?" I urge my brother. *"Kwaku, take Josephine and go."*

He is hesitant to leave me.

"But what about you?!"

My focus is on Abeem, but I still reassure him.

"I will be fine. Josephine matters more than me."

He gives me a surprisingly heartfelt reply.
"Not to me sis, not to me. I am finally getting to know you."
My focus wavers and I meet his eyes.
"It's been nice ey bro? I'll see you soon."

The emotional connection between us these last few days is magical. Still, there is work to do. He gives me a final look of respect. He then escorts Josephine out of the arena swiftly.

And with that, I enter the arena to face Abeem. The moment I do, she runs at me full speed. As she does, I go for a leg sweep that she jumps and flips over. Then, she lunges at me with a jumping punch combo. I do a few quick blocks before I return her assault with a couple of kicks of my own. She grabs one of my legs to come quickly come in with a punch that hits my side. However, I twist and spin out of the hold while hitting her head my other foot. We eye each other again. We are an even match. She jumps to me with another kick. I back off from it and weave into a punch combo. She counters my combo with a back elbow. I roll with that into a surprise spinning hook kick. She rolls back from that and lunges for my free leg. The back-and-forth dance continues on the ground. We start wrestling into submission holds when a sharp shock hits my neck. My Surge powers start to freeze from the shock. I look over and see General Aku looming over us. Her control baton continues to stun me. The pain is unbearable as I grab at my neck to feel a Surge dampener collar. She nods with approval to Abeem.

General Aku lords her advantage over me.
"Well well, you must be the special shockhead who started this whole mess in my city. I see that you have freed my Seraph as well. Seems like you are winning this battle. But you'll lose

this war. The first key to this loss is taking out the leader. As that is you, you'll lose your life here eventually. And Abeem, excellent work. I'll be sure to promote you to Colonel. Just think of all the credits there will be for your family as well."

The general continues to shock me several times.
"Your Surge powers have no chance against this. It's a shame you had to kill the brilliant mind of Dr. Boateng. It leaves me saddened. But I'm sure after we research your insides, we'll get more of what we need from the Surge. Plus your body and spirit will be the perfect beacon for the Seraphs."

She dials up the intensity of the pain with a gleam in her eye.
"You shockheads are the bane of my existence. You're the only things stopping a full and complete return of the Asante kingdom in Ghana. If you and even your detective ilk in Accra were gone we could conquer all of West Africa. Vile shockheads."

Abeem tries to reason with the sociopathic nature of General Aku.
"General, I think that's enough. We've got to go check on our troops. They need our help. We can deal with her later."

The general ignores her request.
"Hush Abeem, you've got your promotion, now let me have my fun."

Suddenly, there is a loud bang. The shocks to the dampener subside. I take a moment of reprieve before I can function again. My eyes hover over to Abeem holding a smoking vibro-rifle. I line up her target and see General Aku clutching her chest.

Her mouth is agape. She is in disbelief at Abeem's choice.
"But Abeem…why? They're just lower-class Surge shockheads."

Fuming with anger and sadness, Abeem berates the general.
"That's my friend and ex-lover. I don't need your help for my family. Fuck you fAku, you're a tyrant not a general!"

She fires another round into the general. She slumps dead from the shot.

Finally becoming aware of myself, I talk to Abeem.
"Abeem, there's no way they'll let you live with this."
She shrugs and helps me to my feet.
"No. I don't think anyone will care that this bitch is gone. Now, what was it you said about charges before Josephine and that other guy left?"
I give her a look of concern but continue with the information she needs.
"That was my brother Kwaku. He set explosive charges throughout the stronghold."
With surprise, she shows a small smile.
"O so you've reconnected. Well, if you all set those charges, then we've got to go. As for the military, let me worry about that."

Abeem and I run out of the stronghold. The charge timers go off one by one. The structure explodes and crumbles around us. We barely make it out in time. We take a glance at the ruins and we're thankful to be alive. We hear cheers surrounding us. The military is in chains, the military vehicles and weapons are ours, and the stronghold is no more. The Regiment and slum-dwellers shout with pride. Amongst the celebration, a couple of Regiment aim their Surge powers at Abeem.

I step in front of her and open my arms to block them.
"Hold on, she's a friend."

I focus on her.
"I hope?"
She agrees and addresses the crowd.
"Yes Afia, I am. Greetings everyone, I'm Colonel Abeem and I'll be running this establishment from here on out. I will protect you as human beings not as the lower class. We will begin to demilitarize the Asante kingdom. Instead, we will use our resources in aiding and protecting you. Take off those shackles fellow Surge people. You are welcome here. And if the military has an issue with all of this then they can deal with my new Surge recruits."
The Regiment acknowledges her request. With their approval, she continues.
"If you'll join me we can make a difference. This work won't be easy, but we can make Ghana a better place."
I place a hand on her shoulder in solidarity.
"Abeem, thank the Orishas you're back."
She hugs me with peace.
"It's good to be back Afia! This will be a lot of work, but now I can help my family directly. I'm so sorry about us."
I embrace her back.
"It's fine Abeem." I then realize I forgot about Josephine.
"Josephine! Let me tend to Josephine!"

I see my brother and Xochitl propping up a weak Josephine. I rush to their side.

I ask Kwaku about her condition.
"How is she doing?"
He regretfully explains how Josephine is.
"She's fading Afia."
She opens her eyes and tells me what will happen to her.
"Afia, I will be joining the ether soon. It is a reconnection to the synchronicity to become the Surge itself. The Seraphs have

reached out and know that I will be coming. Do you wish to join me?"

Her request sounds impossible.
"That's not even possible. Is it Josephine?"
She explains more details.
"When the Seraphs reach out, before we go to the ether, we may take one with us. The reason is to strengthen the Surge and our people. Ultimately, it is up to you."
Xochitl encourages the journey for me.
"You should go Afia; we'll be ok here."
I thank her, but then I stare at my brother.
"Thank you. But what about you brother, I just reconnected with you. I finally made peace with you. And what about Abeem and the rebuilding and the Surge candidates." .
My big brother quiets me and comforts me.
"Afia, relax. You must do this to see for yourself what happens. You may find more Seraphs, or you may return to us. No matter what, the Surge will always be with us. If the Surge is with us, then you will be too. You have always loved adventure. And this is a journey that I think you'll love. Yes, I love you for the first time in ages, but this is bigger than that. So you have to be on your way now."

Tears pool in my eyes while I hug him. I hug Xochitl too. Abeem comes over to us.

She gives her words of encouragement as well.
"Afia, we will be fine. You've helped us more than you could have ever known. And I'm going to miss you my love. Maybe we'll date again sometime."
My tears flow freely now. My voice shakes when I speak.
"Yeah…that would be nice. Real nice."

Abeem comes in close and holds me for a long time. She kisses me with tears running down her cheek. I wipe them off her and hold her chin up. We both smile at each other for possibly the last time.

Josephine signals for me that it is time.
"Afia, it is time. And my dear, you are not dying. You are becoming a part of the Surge. Who knows what the Seraphs and the Surge hold for us."
I face her and concede to her wisdom.
"Alright Josephine, show me a new world."

I hold Josephine's hand. Angelic light surrounds us. I see my old mentor, Lacuna's, visage reaching out. I am so happy to see her again. I hold her hand with my other. Xochitl sees Lacuna's outline and gasps. Lacuna, Josephine and I fade into the atmosphere. We become one with the ether of the Surge and the Seraphs.

END